SMASH
THE WILD BUNCH

SMASH THE WILD BUNCH

Giles A. Lutz

Thorndike Press • Thorndike, Maine

W
L.T.

Library of Congress Cataloging in Publication Data:

Lutz, Giles A.
  Smash the wild bunch.

  1. Large type books. I. Title.
[PS3562.U83S6 1982b]   813'.54 82-16838
ISBN 0-89621-408-7

Large Print edition available through arrangement with Walker and Company.

Cover design by Armen Kojoyian.

SMASH
THE WILD BUNCH

CHAPTER 1

Marshal Evett Nix cursed with all the passion
in his being as another bead of sweat dropped
from his forehead, blotting the words he was
trying to write. He'd have enough trouble
without sending his superior officer an unreadable letter. He clenched his fist and smashed it
down on the desk. He wasn't on the best of
footing with Washington. Sending a blurry,
blotched report would just about finish him.
He had been working on the letter most of the
morning and he hadn't turned out a decent
copy yet. The crumpled balls of paper were
mounting in the wastepaper basket. He was
squeezed mercilessly between the unbearable
weather and the pressure from Washington.
He had spent most of yesterday trying to
answer what he was doing about capturing and
jailing the Wild Bunch. With the passing of

each unsuccessful day, the pressure from Washington grew worse. Washington didn't realize or care about the difficulties he faced. Bill Doolin and his bunch were probably the worst outlaws Oklahoma had ever known. The Dalton gang had been bad, but Doolin was beginning to outdistance them in notoriety. Capturing Doolin and his outlaws was about as easy as trying to hold a handful of smoke. Each time Nix was hopeful of seeing success, that unruly bunch slipped through his fingers. He had tried to tell Washington what he faced. Oklahoma was a wild, untamed land with uncounted hiding places. Once Doolin pulled off a new job, he simply vanished. Part of the trouble was that much of this part of the country was sympathetic to Doolin and his gang. People gave him shelter, food, and protection. Doolin's escapades had made him a kind of hero to too many people. He had tried to explain that to Washington, and Washington hadn't been interested. Washington demanded results. If the job was too big for Nix to handle, somebody who would do the job could be found.

Nix groaned, stood, and wandered about the office. This goddamned job was hard enough without him having to answer those quick-springing suspicions in Washington. Lately he had gotten so that his fingers trembled each time he opened an official letter from Washington, fearful that he would read the announcement of his being replaced by another man. He was a proud man, and he had worked hard to justify his appointment. That didn't mean anything to Washington. If he couldn't cut the job, Washington would find someone else who could. To those bureaucrats it was as simple as that. Sending them a blotched, blurry letter would only solidify their suspicions that his position as chief marshal of Oklahoma was too big for him.

He mopped his face again. It wasn't yet ten o'clock this morning, and already his handkerchief was sodden. His shirt clung damply to his torso. A man couldn't keep enough fresh shirts in this climate to stay comfortable. He had changed shirts this morning, and he was down to his last one. The damned laundry was slow as usual, and all his rantings and ravings couldn't budge them a whit. The laundry bills were eating him alive. "Goddamned weather," he muttered. He wished Washington had to work a summer in Oklahoma. He'd like to see how those desk-riding clerks could stand that.

He grinned wanly. That would never happen. But facing the rest of the summer was a reality. It was only July, and the heat was bearing down like a great, moist blanket, bearing down until a man thought he couldn't get his breath. He crossed to the bucket of drinking water, removing the cover before he reached for the dipper. He got only a scant mouthful of water down before he flung the remains across the office. He had changed to drinking water this morning, and it wasn't fit to drink. It had a flat, brackish taste, and man's thirst had to be bad for him to be able to drink this stuff.

That unleashed his passion again, and he cursed with all the vehemence in his being. It was childish to let go like this, but he was pushed beyond his endurance.

"If you want all of Guthrie to hear you, you're succeeding," a voice said from the doorway.

Nix whirled, his face flaming. His pride extended to his appearance and to the way he did his job, and it was embarrassing to be caught in a moment of weakness like this.

His face relaxed as he saw the tall, rangy man in the doorway. "Oh, it's you, Frank," he muttered. He stalked over to his desk and reseated himself. He wasn't even going to explain a moment of weakness like this.

Frank Grimes came into the office. He was in his late twenties, but his face looked too tired for his years. When he grinned, there was

10

no merriment in it. Stress rode him too hard.

He sat down across from Nix. It eased Nix's strain; this man showed he was carrying his share of troubles. "Hello, Frank," he said, his voice lightening. Here was as good a man as had ever worked for him. Grimes had quit four years ago, and nothing Nix could say would dissuade him. Grimes's heart had been wrapped up in those eighty acres he had been buying. He couldn't leave quick enough.

The quirk of humor remained on Grimes's lips. "You look like you've been ridden too hard and put away wet," he drawled.

"You came close to calling it," Nix growled. "I can't even write a letter to Washington without sweating all over it." He gestured at the half-filled wastebasket. "Look at that. Before I can finish the letter, I sweat all over it and ruin it."

Grimes chuckled. "I've got two solutions for you. Wait until night to write it or wait until winter comes."

"Brilliant," Nix said bitterly. "If I'm a day late, Washington chews my ass out."

"Must be important for Washington to get so worked up," Grimes commented.

"As far as I'm concerned, it's the most important matter I've ever handled. My job could hang on it."

Grimes looked at him with renewed interest. He had worked for Nix for four years before he had resigned. He had known a calm, unperturbed man with nothing so drastic that he lost time worrying over it. This wasn't the same man at all.

"Come on, Evett," he protested. "Aren't you building it up a little?"

Nix's eyes began to refire. "Building it up, the man claims," he yelled. "All I've got on my back is the damned weather, then Washington." He gestured wildly. "Right behind those two things comes Bill Doolin. Was he kicking up his particular brand of hell when you carried a badge, Frank?"

"I never saw him, but I've seen enough posters to know what he looks like," Grimes replied. "I thought he rode with the Dalton gang. Didn't that bunch get wiped out in the Coffeyville raid?"

"Doolin was lucky or blessed by the devil. He and Bob Dalton got into some kind of an argument before that Coffeyville raid. Bob Dalton kicked him out. Doolin missed the raid that could have cost him his life. I guess riding with the Daltons taught him a taste for easy living without working for it. He started up his own bunch. That bunch is raising far more hell than the Daltons ever did. Think of any devil-

12

ment the Daltons caused, and Doolin's gang has doubled it. Hell, don't you ever read the papers?"

"Not very often," Grimes confessed. "I've been too busy to be interested in what's going on in the world."

Nix sighed. "You're a lucky man, Frank. Not to have this mess on your back."

"Washington was always a skinflint boss," Grimes said dryly. "When I worked for you, you were always complaining about them not giving you enough money or enough men to get the job done."

"It's different this time," Nix said bitterly. "You wouldn't believe it, but I've got a hundred deputies working for me. That's enough men to cover Oklahoma like a blanket. No, this time Washington has been overgenerous. Their big beef now is the lack of results. Even with all those men, I can't get a single solid lead on Doolin and the Wild Bunch." His face was pinched tight from some inner distress. "It's liable to cost me my job," he finished.

Grimes shook his head. "Damned if you don't sound whipped. I never saw you like this. Doolin is just a man, with no more powers than any other man."

Nix breathed hard. "You sound just like some of the letters Washington sends me. How would you go about unearthing him?"

Grimes tilted back his head and looked at the ceiling. His head didn't move for a long moment while he reflected. "I'd send a posse after him, as many men as it takes to do the job. That shouldn't be any problem if you've got as many men as you claim."

Nix sagged back in his chair. He didn't actually throw up his hands, but he gave that impression. "I've tried that a dozen times. You think he hasn't powers more than any ordinary man. You should have been on his tail. One minute he's right ahead of you, the next he vanishes completely."

"No man can do that," Grimes stated in flat disbelief.

"You think not? Half of the people in this state think he's some kind of a hero. They're happy to hide him. They enjoy seeing the law stumbling over its own feet. Do you know I've lost ten men to Doolin's bullets? He's fast and smart. On top of that, he's deadly. So is every man who rides with him. Informers all over the state tell Doolin every move this office makes. He lays an ambush for my posses and cuts them to pieces. If he ever suspects one of my deputies is on his tail, he cuts him down."

"He's really got you treed, hasn't he?" Grimes commented.

14

Nix resented that remark, but he couldn't deny the truth. "He has so far. But I'll get him. One way or another."

Silence fell between the two. Grimes was sorry for an old friend, but he didn't see where he could do anything to change the situation. The silence grew oppressive, and to break the silence he asked, "How does a man like Doolin get started out against law and order? Did he start out bad as a kid?"

"The funny part is that he didn't. He was as hard-working a kid as ever grew up. He established quite a reputation as a cowhand. Then one day he did a complete flip-over."

"Something had to happen to change him," Grimes insisted.

"It did," Nix admitted. "It happened during a Fourth of July celebration. A bunch of cowboys held the celebration in a grove of trees a quarter of a mile out of town. Somebody decided beer would give the celebration some life and they collected several beer kegs and sawed them in two. After filling the halves with ice, they stuck beer bottles into the ice. The celebration was going good when a couple of constables appeared and demanded that the celebration be stopped."

Grimes's eyebrows shot up. "Why? They weren't doing any harm."

"Those constables didn't think so. You see, Doolin and the others had stepped over the state line in selecting that piece of timber. They were in Kansas, and Kansas is a dry state. No one would admit ownership of the beer, but that didn't stop the constables. They said they'd have to confiscate the beer. Doolin warned them to leave the beer alone. That started an argument, and the argument led to a gun fight. The two constables were badly wounded. It was never learned whether or not Doolin started the fight, or even wounded the lawmen. But he was blamed for the incident. 'Wanted' posters went out for him. From then on, he had to be on the dodge."

Grimes scowled. "You mean all this trouble started from an overzealous act of the constables?"

Nix nodded.

"That goddamned stupid petty law of Kansas. That's what started Doolin bad?"

Again, Nix nodded. "That was only the start. Doolin shot his way out of several attempts to take him. Each time he was successful his reputation grew. A few daring men joined him, seeing the quality of leadership in him. Those men had to be fed and supplied. There was only one way to get that money. Doolin pulled off a train robbery. The 'wanted' posters grew.

Doolin was pushed into more daring attempts. More train robberies followed, then several bank robberies. Each success pulled more daring men to him. Now I've got this mess on my hands."

"Unbelievable how stupidity can build a mistake into a major problem," Grimes said. "If it hadn't been for those two constables, Doolin might still be a hard-working, law-abiding man."

Nix grinned twistedly. "That'll always be debatable. Doolin could have been born with that reckless streak in him. No one will ever be able to say."

"Evett, do you really think you can capture Doolin and his bunch?"

"My commission says I have to," Nix said wearily. "Anyway, what I just told you explains how Doolin's wild bunch got started. I guess Doolin got a taste for leadership of reckless men, and he liked it. His bunch seems to have grown steadily. When he lost one to the law, there were always a couple more to take the place of the lost one. Maybe he found out working for a living had less appeal than just grabbing for what he wanted. I'll capture him," he finished. "If Washington gives me enough time." He said that in so low a voice that Grimes barely caught it. "Every letter I get from those people shows how more impatient they're getting. I was trying to write that I got a report that Doolin and his Wild Bunch have been seen around Ingalls."

Grimes frowned. "I've never heard of that town."

"That's no surprise. It's only a dot on the map. Not more than a hundred and fifty people live around it, though it's located on some pretty good farming land."

"Maybe I should have gone to Ingalls in the first place," Grimes said bitterly.

The bitterness brought Nix to the realization that other men had problems, maybe as severe as the one he faced. "Things going bad, Frank?"

"Couldn't be worse," Grimes said gloomily. "I just came back from the bank. Shelton refused to extend my note. This goddamned weather finished me." He cursed the weather with the same passion Nix had shown earlier. "All of my crops burned up. Even my water source dried up. I had to sell the few head of livestock I had. They went at distress prices." He shrugged. "This year comes on top of two bad ones. I didn't lose any money, but I didn't make any either. Evett, for the first time in my life I begged another man to give me a break. That damned Shelton just sat there stony-faced. A payment was due, and I couldn't make it. I walked out of that bank stripped of everything. Why in the hell did I ever think I wanted to be a farmer? I remember you warned me. But no, I was obsessed with raising things. I quit a solid job to give farming a fling." He sat there in gloomy retrospection for a moment, then shrugged again. "What the hell. It's no skin off your nose. I was just passing your office, and I came in to burden your ear with my woes." That twisted grin flashed again.

"And I beat you to the punch by dumping my woes on you," Nix said, and chuckled bleakly. "I guess we're proving to each other that the other man doesn't have such a good thing. What are you going to do, Frank?"

"I'll be damned if I know," Grimes said with open candor. "Want to take back a not-so-good deputy and a busted farmer?" He raised a hand, stopping Nix's effort to speak. "Forget I said that, Evett. I'm not down to begging yet."

Nix's eyes picked up a new fire, and he leaned forward. "Why shouldn't I give you a job, Frank? I need a good, reliable man. One that the Doolin gang won't recognize at sight. You could ride to Ingalls and report back to me if there's any truth in the rumor that Doolin is hanging out around Ingalls. He doesn't know

19

you. He wouldn't up and shoot you on sight. I'm not imagining that," he said bleakly. "I've lost deputies that way before."

Grimes sat there, his face so impassive that Nix knew he was going to refuse the offer. "I couldn't take it, Evett. I've got Chad on my hands."

Nix had forgotten about Chad. Chad was man-sized, but still a kid in age. "Sure," he said in quick understanding. "How old is Chad now?"

"Nineteen," Grimes answered. "Four years younger than me. When Pa died eight years ago, I promised him I'd keep an eye out for Chad until he was grown up. Well, he hasn't grown up yet. There's still a streak of kid in him. Maybe it's my fault. Maybe I didn't do such a good job." That wasn't self-accusation in his tone; he spoke like a man who looked over the job he had done and calmly accepted his findings. "So you see, I couldn't go off and just leave him. I wouldn't be sure of what he might get into."

"Not Chad," Nix said in quick protest.

Grimes shook his head. "Maybe somebody once felt the same way about Bill Doolin. But he turned bad when he got into the right circumstances. I'm going to be damned sure that nothing like that ever happens to Chad."

Nix sat there, his fingertips drumming on his desk. He wasn't going to take Grimes's refusal. This could be the solution he had been seeking.

"Take him with you. Why not?" he asked, stopping Grimes's outbreak. "It'd make your cover that much better. The two of you would be just a couple of farmers, looking over some new prospects. If Doolin is at Ingalls, his suspicions wouldn't be aroused. I couldn't put Chad on full pay, but I could see that he's paid something. The two of you might even be able to save something."

He saw the fire return to Grimes's eyes. "We might be able to work something out, Evett."

Nix's face cleared. Grimes was bending his way. "Is Chad around?"

"He's in town somewhere."

"Good," Nix said heartily. "Find him and bring him back. The three of us could talk it over. Chad might be interested."

Grimes stood and walked to the door. He turned there and said gruffly, "I can't thank you enough, Evett."

"For what?" Nix scoffed.

"For giving me a new chance." Grimes made no attempt to hide the hope springing to life in his eyes.

Nix made a denying slash of his hand.

"Think of what you could be doing for me. Go on and see if you can find Chad and bring him back."

Grimes went out of the door with a new spring to his step. He was so engrossed in his thoughts that he paid no attention to the ragged, nondescript characters standing across the street. It was funny how life turned out. He had walked into Nix's office as low as a man could get, and he had walked out with something that gave him new spirit. Nix's offer reached down and lifted him out of his despondency. Sure, what he could be doing would help Nix but, most of all, he would be helping himself. He lengthened his stride, whistling as he walked.

Ragged Bill watched him go on down the street, his eyes narrowing. He hadn't the slightest idea of who this stranger could be, or why he had been so long in Marshal Nix's office. But it might be interesting to Bill Doolin. Better, it could do something for himself. If he brought Doolin some interesting information, it would put him in good standing with the Wild Bunch. If Doolin accepted him into the Wild Bunch, it would mean a better life for him. He could live better; he could afford some decent clothes, and his belly would always be filled. His mouth filled with saliva. His hands trembled with anticipation. God, he had tried so hard to win Doolin's appreciation. Maybe this would do it.

He settled down with his back against a post that supported the metal awning of the grocery store. He could sit here for a long time without anybody giving him a second look. Maybe that stranger would come back, and he would have something else to report to Doolin. Flies crawled over his face and hands, and he didn't even bother to shoosh them away. He was used to those minor irritations. A tramp dog came up and sniffed at him, and the ragged man thought the dog might lift his leg.

"Get out of here," he hissed.

The dog jerked in alarm and jumped straight up in the air. It landed a pace from the ragged man, its tongue lolling out. It slowly walked away, twice turning its head to look back at the seated man. Maybe there was some harm in that pile of rags.

That damned dog learned in a hurry. It gave balm to the ragged man's soul. If this turned out as he planned, he would have respect from more than just a tramp dog; he would have respect from people.

CHAPTER 2

Grimes searched three saloons before he found Chad. He walked into the Last Trick Saloon and stood for a moment in the doorway, frowning at the familiar back. A mug of beer was before Chad and, as Grimes watched, Chad lifted the mug and took a long swallow from it. There was nothing wrong in that, but Nix's story of Doolin drinking beer that had started him on the road to ruin stuck in Grimes's mind. There was no parallel in the two characters. Chad was a good kid, and drinking a beer wasn't shoving him into the ranks of lawbreakers, but it could happen. There was an air of recklessness about him. Nothing could develop it more than boredom.

Grimes shook away the momentary illusion. He was going to be damned sure that nothing like what happened to Doolin would ever happen to Chad. He walked up to Chad and tapped him on the shoulder.

Chad whirled, his face tightening for an instant at the sight of his brother. "Don't go judging me," Chad said. "I was just drinking a beer. There was nothing else to do while I waited for you."

Grimes let the remark go, though he was sure it was more than a beer. Only the bartender and another customer were in the room. Grimes wanted to talk to his brother without being overheard.

"Come with me," he said. "I want to talk to you."

Neither of them spoke until they stepped out onto the street. Then Chad said, "That goddamned bank turned you down."

"What makes you say that?"

"It's written all over your face." Chad was a full head taller than Grimes, but the lanky frame hadn't yet filled out. His stringy muscles would develop with a little more maturity. He wasn't a handsome man, though there was an appeal to the blue eyes with the tow-colored hair stringing down over them. The square jaw was massive, probably the most outstanding feature of his face.

Chad had a keen perception. "I knew you'd be turned down." He unleashed a string of bitter oaths. "We're honest. We would have made the farm pay. If only they gave us a little more time. Those damned people wouldn't trust anybody! There's too many bankers in this world. The only way to handle that kind is to walk in with a gun and take what you need."

There was that streak of recklessness showing. In his wildness, Chad was almost willing to try anything.

It wasn't said rationally, but a man could brood over a real or imagined wrong until that streak of wildness grew and blotted everything else. The thought of Bill Doolin flashed into Grimes's mind. Maybe Doolin had been so squeezed into a corner that he could no longer think straight. Maybe he had felt like Chad did at the beginning.

Grimes gripped Chad's arm, and his fingers bit deep. "Stop that kind of talk," he said sharply. "Yes, I got turned down. They took the farm. Don't blame the bankers. We failed to meet an obligation. We didn't do our job right, or we would have been able to meet that payment. Can you blame the bank for the weakness that was in us? I knew what could happen when I signed for that loan. It happened. I lost the farm, but that's the law. It broke us. It happens that way."

Chad wasn't to be pacified. "I'd like to point a gun at that banker's head and see how he reacts. Maybe that wouldn't be his fault, but this damned weather wasn't our fault either."

Grimes's fingers dug deeper. "I told you to stop that kind of talk." His voice had grown sharper. He knew how Chad felt. Things were closing in on him, and he was lashing out blindly. He wasn't old enough to see that this kind of thinking would only dig deeper the hole he was already in.

"You ready to talk some sense?" Grimes asked.

Chad nodded, and Grimes let up on the pressure of his fingers. "After I left the bank, I stopped by to talk to Marshal Nix," Grimes went on. "You remember him?"

"Sure I do. You used to work for him. Though that was quite a while back. I didn't see him often. The farm kept me too busy." His voice remained steady enough.

"That was my trouble too," Grimes said. "My attention was too absorbed in my own doings to realize that other people had their troubles too. Washington is on Evett's tail to stop Bill Doolin. You've heard of him?"

"The famous outlaw." Chad showed more interest. "I've heard about him, though I never saw him. Maybe he had a reason for what he's doing. Maybe he was pushed into it. He's showing the world that he can get along without it. He's worked out a simple method. Whatever he wants or needs he takes."

Grimes sighed. "You've got a lot of wild ideas in your head. Some way I'm going to have to drive them out. You said a while back that nobody cares what happens to anybody else. You're dead wrong. Evett Nix cares. He's breaking his butt to take care of all the little people who are being trampled by more powerful men. Without people like Nix, it'd really be a jungle with the strong eating up the weak." Oh God, he thought fervently, Chad's already thinking along the wrong lines. He had to find a way to get all those poisonous thoughts out of Chad's head.

"Don't say anything," he said as Chad started to speak. "Just listen. Nix's offered both of us jobs. I'll go back on the payroll at full scale. He can't put you on as a regular marshal, but both of us will be earning money."

Some of the tight strain left Chad's face, and his eyes didn't have that wild glitter. "You mean we're back working? At what?"

Here came the difficult part. Only a moment ago, Chad had been talking favorably about Bill Doolin. Now Grimes was going to ask him to assist in the capture of Doolin. "Nix got a report that Doolin has been seen around Ingalls. He can't send any of his regular

28

deputies out there to check up because Doolin knows most of them. But he doesn't know us. We're to go out there to look over some new farming land. Doolin won't suspect us. If he's out there, we'll report back to Evett. How does it sound to you?"

He waited for resentment to flash across Chad's face, but it didn't come. Chad was visibly excited. "You mean we'd be instrumental in capturing Doolin. Hell, Frank, there might even be a reward in it."

Grimes didn't grin openly. That was the mercurial disposition of kids. One moment their thoughts were firmly fixed on one thing, then the next they flipped over completely. "You've got it," he said heartily.

"It sounds good to me, Frank. For the first time in a long while, we'll have some money coming in. That'll be a welcome change. You know that damned farm was beginning to wear me out. We put out all that work and got nothing in return."

Grimes chuckled with pleasure. Give a kid a new idea to fasten onto and his thinking completely changes.

Chad lengthened his stride, and Grimes caught up with him and asked in mild irritation, "Why all the hurry?"

"We oughta get back there as fast as we can

to be sure Nix doesn't change his mind."

Grimes thought of the harassment in Nix's voice. "He won't change." He quickened his pace to keep up with Chad; he wasn't going to argue with him.

Chad saw the ragged man sitting with his back against an awning support. "What's he doing here?" he asked.

Grimes frowned as his attention was diverted toward the ragged man. "Why do you ask? Do you know him?"

Chad shook his head. "Never saw him before. By the looks of him, he's a bum. There's getting to be a lot of them in Guthrie."

This was an excellent opportunity to drive home a few telling points, and Grimes seized it. "It looks like there's three classes of people in the world." He paused as Chad's eyebrows shot up. "The bums who beg for their living, the outlaws who use force to take what they need, and the men who work for their living. Only the last have any respect for themselves. Which one would you pick?"

Chad frowned at Grimes's grin. "That's a damn fool question. If a man doesn't have any respect for himself, he's sunk pretty low."

"Good," Grimes said. Chad hadn't lost his ability to think rationally. He put a final glance on the ragged man. Had he seen him before? If so, the man didn't make enough impression for him to remain in Grimes's memory. But he could be grateful to him for one thing: that he was around for Grimes to use him in his object lesson to Chad.

They walked into Nix's office, and Nix sprang to his feet at the sight of them. "Chad," he said, shaking Chad's hand. He looked up into Chad's face. "Do you know how long it's been since I've seen you? My God, you've really sprung up. You don't know how insignificant it makes me feel. Frank tell you what I have in mind?"

"He said something about it."

"Fine," Nix said. "I'm going to put you down at half wages. Maybe later I can do a little better."

"Don't fret about it," Chad said calmly. "I'm just grateful to have something on my hands. You want to give me more explanation that Frank didn't?"

"You know it's Bill Doolin I'm after?"

Chad nodded, and Nix went on. "He's become the scourge of Oklahoma — him and the lice that have gathered around him. There's a class of men who think it's a mark of standing to be able to ride with a well-known outlaw. They never think ahead to realize that when that outlaw goes down they go down too.

31

My deputies know what most of them look like, but they can't get close to any of them without someone pulling a gun and shooting them down. This office has already lost too many good men. I've spent quite a few years in law work, but I think this bunch is the worst I've ever run across."

He abruptly clamped his lips together and sat down at his desk. He had a thick sheaf of pictures on the desk top, and he pushed them toward Grimes and Chad. "This is to help you recognize the Wild Bunch when you run across them. The first one is Bill Doolin."

Grimes barely glanced at the picture, then pushed it over to Chad. Chad studied it intently. It was a good picture of a dark-complexioned man with wide-spaced, gray eyes. Even in a picture, they seemed to gaze broodingly out at the world. The nose was on the prominent side, but it gave character to the face. Not much could be told about the mouth, for a bushy moustache hid most of it. But the chin was audacious and firm, rising above a thick neck.

Chad finally looked up and handed the picture back to Nix. "He looks like a tough character."

"Don't ever take him lightly," Nix said tersely. "He's even tougher than he looks. And deadlier than a rattlesnake." That tight, pinched look returned to his lips. It always did when Doolin was under discussion. "My God, if you knew how many train and bank robberies he's pulled off. I don't blame Washington for getting upset at his depredations. They're demanding that I bring him in. It's a hell of a lot easier saying it than doing it. He's got eyes like a hawk and the instincts of a hungry deer. It's hard to believe that once he was a hard-working, respectable man. Half of Oklahoma lives in trembling fear that he'll hit them next. The other half hero-worships him; they give him shelter whenever he needs it. That makes it really rough to get a lead on him."

"You expect Frank and me to get that lead?" Chad asked.

"Hoping, not expecting," Nix corrected. "Quite a few men have lost their lives trying to hem him in. I want you to use the utmost caution. Don't barge in blindly or you could wind up dead. Doolin has the reputation of being the best gunhand that ever entered Oklahoma. You two are just a couple of farmers going to Ingalls to look for new land — no more than that. Just keep your eyes open. If you get a whisper of the Wild Bunch being around Ingalls, I want you to withdraw and report back to me. No more than that. Under no circumstances are you two to try to take him, even if you think you've got the drop on him. I can't stress that caution too much." He grinned painfully. "That'll do for a start. If I can learn definitely that he's around Ingalls I can send a posse big enough to wipe out that bunch. That'll be accomplishing more than I hoped for." He picked up another picture. "This isn't as clear as Doolin's picture. It's on a 'wanted' poster and blurred." He handed the poster to Grimes. "That's of Oliver Ol Yantis. Study it good. That'll be all you have to go on."

Grimes's eyes fixed on the poster for a long moment. "Ugly-looking cuss," he commented as he handed it to Chad.

"Mean-looking cuss," Chad commented after studying the poster. "He looks like a man would stamp on his head quicker than he would a rattlesnake."

Nix nodded agreement. "That'd be the wisest course. Yantis isn't a big man, and his swarthiness doesn't make him any more appealing. Make no mistake about him. He's almost as good with a gun as Doolin, and just as deadly. Got him fixed in mind?"

Chad and Grimes nodded solemnly. "I'll know him any place I see him," Grimes said in a hard voice.

"Good," Nix said. "This is Bill Dalton." He handed over another poster.

Grimes looked startled. "One of the Dalton boys?" At Nix's nod, he said, "I thought all of the Dalton gang were wiped out in Coffeyville."

"Bill wasn't with them," Nix said. "He made a lot of talk about getting even with the people who shot down his brothers. But it was just talk. He's a big-mouth, but he can still use a gun. Those kind can kill you as quick as any others." He picked up another poster. "This is Bill Blake, alias Tulsa Jack. This one is Charlie Clifton, alias Dan Clifton, alias Dan Wiley, sometimes called Dynamite Jack. Here's George Red Buck Waightman. That's all of the pictures of the Wild Bunch, though I don't doubt there's more of them. More and more are trying to join Doolin. The only thing that will stop these kind is a bullet, or a long jail term. Until they are stopped the killings and robberies will go on. Want to look at these pictures some more?"

Grimes shook his head. "I think I'd know them if I happened to run across them." He glanced at Chad, and Chad nodded.

"I guess that ties up everything," Nix said. "I'd suggest you two drive to Ingalls in a wagon."

Grimes chuckled. "Why? To make us look more farmerish? It's either that, or you don't have any pity for our aching butts. Do you know how much that long a trip takes out of a man's rear?"

Nix laughed. "You'll survive." He stood and shook hands with each man, and he clasped each hand for a long moment. "You just remember what I said about caution. You're not going up there to perform any deeds of daring."

Chad shook his head. "After looking at the pictures of that bunch, I know it knocked any recklessness out of my head. I'm just a farmer looking for land."

Grimes grinned. "You know, I think this boy is learning fast."

He stopped at the door and looked across the street. The ragged man was gone.

"What's bothering you?" Nix asked.

"There was a bum sitting across the street when we came in. He's gone now. I was just wondering if you knew him." He frowned, then shook his head. "It doesn't make any difference. I guess even a bum has to move about some."

"I wish I could have gotten a look at him," Nix fretted. "This kind of business makes a man jumpy."

Grimes laughed. "We'll be nothing more than a couple of farmers looking Ingalls over."

"Just keep it that way," Nix ordered.

CHAPTER 3

Ragged Bill drummed his heels on the mule's bony flanks. No matter how vicious he made the punishment or the length of it, he could only get a few shambling strides before the mule settled back into his dispirited walk. The poor animal really only had two paces; slow and stop.

Ragged Bill swore at the inoffensive animal. He was better than halfway to Ingalls, and he groaned in self-pity as he thought of the punishment lying ahead of him. After he told his story to Doolin, maybe his luck would change. If Doolin would only take him into the Wild Bunch Ragged Bill knew his fortune would change. His share of a successful raid, riding with the Wild Bunch, would buy him a decent horse. He could get rid of this sorry animal. His self-pity grew as he thought of how he had acquired the mule. He had stopped a farmer from slaughtering the animal because of its general uselessness, and he had offered five dollars for it. It had taken every cent in his pocket, and the farmer's cupidity wouldn't let him refuse the offer. The purchase had so stripped him that he didn't have enough money to buy a decent saddle. He had tried to make a pad out of a few old rags, but it was hardly adequate. Every step the mule took sent a jolt through his bony frame, and the pad didn't begin to absorb those shocks. Ragged Bill's self-pity grew, and he almost blubbered. He wouldn't be able to walk by the time he reached Ingalls. Maybe riding this mule was better than walking, but it wasn't much better.

Ragged Bill could have cried in sheer relief as Ingalls came into view. Ingalls wasn't much of a town. It lay thirty-five miles northeast of Guthrie and ten miles east of Stillwater, on the east side of Payne County. It didn't have a railroad connection, and barely even had a passable road.

Dr. A. G. McMurty and Robert Beal had founded the town, though it was hard to see why. Each man owned a quarter-section, and they plotted out forty acres from those sections. They had named the budding town after John J. Ingalls, a United States senator from

Kansas. Senator Ingalls had been instrumental in getting Oklahoma opened to settlement, and McMurty and Beal thought he should be honored. The town was laid out to consist eventually of nine full blocks, with seven additional fractions of blocks. Four streets were laid out: Main, Walnut, Ash, and Oak. The streets ran north and south. Four avenues were also laid out: First, Second, Third, and Fourth – running east and west. The growing town was well thought out. The only trouble was that few people came to help it grow. The dream of a town's growth was only in Mc-Murty's and Beal's vision, and it took more than vision to build something solid.

McMurty opened a drugstore and under-taking parlor in a small frame building hastily thrown up at Oak and Second. Beal picked a location on First to open a general store. A. J. Light put in a blacksmith shop on Ash at First, on the wagon road entering the town limits from the west. A block south on the northwest corner of Ash and Second, J. W. Perry opened a dry-goods store, and on the southeast corner of the intersection Jesse Ramsey constructed another building and stocked it with hardware, amplifying it with an implement yard in front of the store.

Ingalls didn't even have a post office. Falls

City, two miles southeast, had a post office that served Ingalls and the surrounding country. That sorry condition existed until McMurty got a grant for a post office, which he placed in the corner of his drugstore.

The struggling town grew – but oh, so slowly. Charley Vaughn opened a saloon across on Ash Street and down from Light's blacksmith stop. Ketchum's boot and harness shop was half a block away. A cotton gin opened, followed by a gristmill, then a flour mill of fifty barrels daily capacity, and another blacksmith. The population had jumped to a hundred and fifty people. Dr. D. R. Pickering opened his office in his home above Second Avenue on the east side of Oak, and Drs. Briggs and D. H. Selph cared for the sick. Old man Ransom opened another saloon with a poker table, with Neil D. Murray serving as the bartender. Ransom built a livery barn on the next lot south. In the center of the intersection stood a town well with a hand pump. The rough watering trough was hewn from a large cottonwood.

The only two-story building in town was the O.K. Hotel, facing south, a half block east on Second, also owned by Ransom, and run by Edith Ellsworth.

There wasn't a lot of entertainment in

Ingalls. Sadie Comley, widow of an old *X Bar X* cowboy, ran a small gaming parlor in her home. She kept several girls around to serve the lustier tastes of her customers. There must have been enough activity to satisfy the women, for they remained. Sadie drove about the county in a fancy rig behind a team of high-stepping bays. She usually wore a plumed hat. The old-timers called her the Belle of the Cimarron.

From its meager start as a trading post of Payne County, Ingalls was doing well; it was well located, sloping enough for the drainage essential to good health and, at the moment, it boasted of twenty-two business houses. The rolling prairie surrounded it, and there was ample bottom land. Council Creek was only two miles northeast, the Cimarron River over six miles southeast; the Little Stillwater ran about three and a half miles west. People who believed in this land swore that it would produce from fifty to seventy-five bushels of corn per acre. Ingalls wasn't a boom town, but its natural resources made it look as though it was worth developing. Ingalls boasted that it would be a city when the ballooning towns of the west had exploded.

There were no legally appointed law officers. So the Wild Bunch were instinctively drawn to it. Doolin had looked over the town site and was pleased by the lack of nosy marshals. He had picked out as a frequent camp an open cave under a large overhang of rocks on Deer Creek, near its meeting with the Cimarron in the Creek Nation. Dunn's homestead, two and a half miles southeast of Ingalls on Council Creek, was another frequent meeting place selected by Doolin. Dunn had built a frame house and made other sound improvements. He had come to this country with little or no money in his pockets; people talked among themselves, speculating how he came up with the money to do all that he did. There was talk in hushed voices that the money came from the outlaws who used the property. Some speculated that Dunn was a part of the many cattle rustlings, but none made that claim openly, not wanting to arouse Dunn's or the outlaws' wrath.

So this small community was well aware of the outlaws' presence, but as long as they didn't bother Ingalls Ingalls didn't bother Doolin and his bunch. It was a mutually satisfying agreement. The outlaws spent their loot freely in Ingalls, and Ingalls, wisely, didn't talk about them.

Ragged Bill drew up at the outskirts of

Ingalls. His butt was sore and aching, but a jubilation was growing within him. He had made it and, with the information he carried, he was sure that this time Doolin would take him in.

He slid down from the back of the worn-out animal and left it in a grassy swale. It could find enough to eat, and water wasn't far away. Ragged Bill didn't give a damn what happened to the mule. He wouldn't need it again. He walked away without a backward glance. Now he would have to locate Doolin or some of the gang. Doolin would listen to him this time.

He found Doolin and four others of the gang in Ransom's Saloon. At his question, Murray the bartender had asked, "Is Bill expecting you?"

Ragged Bill drew a deep breath to quiet his quivering nerves. "He sure is."

"Well, it's your skin," Murray said after a moment's thought. "You know what will happen if you make him mad."

"He won't get mad this time," Ragged Bill said with an assurance he didn't really feel.

Murray jerked his head toward the rear room. "Bill's back there."

Ragged Bill slipped into the back room, forcing his trembling knees to support him. Doolin and the four members of his bunch

44

were playing a few desultory hands of poker.

"Hello, Bill," said Ragged Bill in a quavering voice.

"Not you again," Doolin said. "The last time I saw you, I told you to quit bothering me." He looked at the man to his right and muttered, "He's been pestering me to let him join our gang. Look at him! He hasn't got enough money to buy a pair of pants to cover his ass." He looked at Ragged Bill, and his eyes began to fire. "Get out of here. I won't tell you again."

"Wait," Ragged Bill pleaded. "I've got some important news to tell you."

Doolin half rose, and Buck Waightman seized a forearm and drew him back into his chair. "Don't go popping off, Bill," he said quietly. "You could listen to what he has to say."

Doolin briefly considered Waightman's words, then nodded grudgingly. "Go ahead and speak your mind."

Ragged Bill tried to keep the tremor out of his voice; Doolin had plainly showed his annoyance. Just a little more — Ragged Bill shuddered and cut off the threat. He wouldn't allow himself to think any more about it.

"I happened to be across the street from Marshal Nix's office in Guthrie." He swallowed at the tightening of Doolin's lips. Doolin didn't even like Nix's name to be mentioned. "I didn't have anything to do with Nix," he said hastily, wanting to allay Doolin's quick-springing suspicion. "I just happened to be in the right place at the right time. I saw this stranger walk into Nix's office. I'd never seen him before. He stayed for almost an hour."

"What's so important about that?" Doolin asked with ominous quietness.

"If that had been all, I wouldn't have thought any more about it," Ragged Bill said hurriedly. "But something told me this was going wrong. He wasn't just a casual visitor to Nix. He stayed too long."

Doolin glowered at his pause. "Go on," he snapped.

"I stayed there until that stranger came out. He looked like he had something on his mind. He hurried down the street like he had some purpose. I waited until he came back. He had a younger man with him. They could have been related. They looked a lot alike."

Doolin straightened in his chair. "What's all this crap supposed to mean to me?"

Waightman laid his hand on Doolin's forearm. "Let him finish, Bill."

Ragged Bill licked his lips, and his voice picked up a frantic note. "You know how Nix is always trying to get somebody to see if they can't get a lead on you. Those two strangers could be the ones Nix is planning on sending up here. You don't know them. Seeing them around wouldn't make you suspicious. Then they could get their report to Nix without alarming you."

Doolin settled back in his chair, his face thoughtful. "It could be," he muttered. "What was their names?"

Ragged Bill threw up his hands in a sort of helplessness. "How could I find that out? I didn't dare ask around. I'd never seen either of them before."

That mean, calculating look was returning to Doolin's eyes. "You know what I think? I think you're making up all of this stuff to impress me."

Ragged Bill's worry increased. "Why would I do that?" he asked frantically.

"In the hopes that it'd make me consider taking you into the bunch," Doolin said with brutal candor. Then something occurred to him. "You can describe them, can't you?"

"I guess I can do that," Ragged Bill said doubtfully. He squinched up his eyes, trying to recall a mental picture of the two men he had seen in Guthrie. He wanted to wail that he had only caught a glimpse of them, but he was wiser than to do something foolish like that.

Doolin was already half angry.

"Let me see. Both men were tall. The shorter one was at least six feet. The younger one was a good head taller. Both of them had a sunburned look like they'd spent a lot of time outside. They were used to working hard, for neither carried any extra weight. Not good looking," he said hopefully, fighting to recall the tiniest shred of what he knew. "Both highcheekboned, giving them a raw look. I'd say they were tough enough for anything they had to face." His mind was empty, and he asked fearfully, "Is that enough?" He thought of one last item and added, "I think they'll always be together."

"That's just fine," Doolin said sarcastically. "I could pick them out easy in a crowd of two."

Waightman stepped in. Doolin was rapidly working himself up. "It could be helpful, Bill," he suggested. "Nix could be trying to slip a couple of strangers into Ingalls. Maybe he's done us a favor."

Doolin frowned at Ragged Bill. "He never did a favor for anybody in his life. Do you think this handful of guesses is enough for me to take you into the bunch?"

"I was only trying to be helpful," Ragged Bill whined. He was getting a tight feeling in his throat. He didn't like the way Doolin was looking at him. "I could be a lot of use to you. I'm tough enough to do anything you wanted."

Waightman laughed, a mean burst of sound. "You're tough?" he asked derisively. "Name one time when you were tough."

Ragged Bill's mind was one empty voice. He couldn't think of a single instance where he had been tough. Then it came to him: a pitiful little incident that might do. "I knocked an old man in the head in Stillwater," he boasted. "I took forty dollars off of him. All he had."

Doolin's eyes turned wild. "What was that old man's name?" he asked in a choked voice.

"Walters or something like that. I didn't stay around to find out."

"Could it be Walthers?" Doolins asked in a silky voice.

"It could be," Ragged Bill replied. "As I told you, I didn't stay around to find out."

"So it was Walthers," Doolin said. He was having trouble in getting the words out. He shook off Waightman's restraining hand and stood. His face was a mask of fury. "So you were the one," he snapped. "I always wanted to know who killed him. Walthers did me a hell of a favor several years ago. I've always kept my eyes open to find a way to repay him." The gun literally jumped into his hand, and its muzzle centered on Ragged Bill's chest. "You worthless little bastard," he ground out as he pulled the trigger once, then again.

Ragged Bill's face froze with rank terror at the appearance of the gun. He tried to say something, and his tongue froze in his mouth. He did manage to raise a pleading hand before Doolin shot. The bullets slammed into his chest, knocking him back a couple of steps before he fell. He didn't move after that. He looked nothing more than a careless pile of rags.

The other men in the room stared wonderingly at Doolin. Only Waightman dared express his wonder. It had all happened so quick that it was difficult to gather his thoughts and put them into order so that he could speak.

"Why, Bill?" he asked, and there might have been a tinge of reproach in his voice. "He was trying to do you a favor."

"Favor, hell," Doolin snarled. "He killed an old man I liked."

Waightman shook his head. "I didn't mean that. I was referring to the information he tried to give you."

Doolin still seethed. "Probably not worth a damn."

"You won't just overlook it," Waightman said incredulously. "There could be something to it."

Doolin walked toward the door, passing the body on the floor. He didn't even glance at it. "Oh, I'll remember what he said. If I see anybody like he described, I'll find out about them. I don't even think those two strangers will ever appear in Ingalls."

"You think he was lying?" Waightman asked.

"I wouldn't put anything past that bastard," Doolin snapped. "The only thing he wanted was to be taken into the bunch." He opened the door and called, "Murray, come here."

Murray came into the room, his face a little tight. He had heard the shots, but gunfire was nothing new in Ingalls. He glanced at the body on the floor and asked casually, "Trouble, Bill?"

"Not really," Doolin said carelessly. "We couldn't see eye to eye."

"I shouldn't have let him in," Murray said, worried.

"Don't fret about it," Doolin reassured him. "Get rid of this garbage, will you?"

"You know I will, Bill."

"I knew you would, Murray." He extended a hand.

Murray thought Doolin wanted to shake hands, and he reached out. Doolin's hand barely touched his before Doolin left the room. The others trailed after him. Murray looked at his hand after they left. His eyes rounded in wonder at the size of the bill in it. Nobody ever suffered at doing what Doolin wanted.

CHAPTER 4

During the last four miles to Ingalls, Chad was shifting from one cheek to the other to ease his aching butt.

Grimes grinned with grim amusement. He knew how Chad felt — his own butt was sore and tender.

"Couldn't you have picked a more comfortable seat?" Chad growled.

Grimes hawked and spat over a wheel. "You don't have much choice in farm wagons. They weren't built for pleasure riding."

Nix had helped select the wagon. It was old and showing the wear of much hard use. One of the wheels had a flat spot on it and besides the jolt when it reached that spot, it squealed dolefully with each turn.

"That goddamned wheel is going to drive me out of my mind," Chad complained bitterly.

"Can't we do anything to stop that squealing?"

"If that's the worst we have to endure on this trip, I'll be grateful," Grimes said soberly. "Maybe we can get it attended to after we reach Ingalls."

"Are you planning on using this wreck some more?" Chad asked indignantly. He started to add further condemnation, but that racking cough broke up his words. He had been coughing a couple of days before his trip started and, along the way, it had grown worse.

"We've got to have something to get around in," Grimes said practically. "Unless you want to walk. I hope this miserable town has a doctor."

"Why do you want a doctor?"

"To get you something for that cough."

"Well, it'll go away. It's only the aftermath of a summer cold," Chad said heatedly.

"Do you want it to go into pneumonia?"

"That might be a welcome change after this trip," Chad answered moodily.

Grimes shook his head. "You're really down, aren't you?" He made a sweeping bend in the road, and the small town of Ingalls suddenly rose out of the prairie. "There she is," he said. "Ingalls, the queen of the prairie."

Chad found no humor in what he saw. "How long do you think we'll have to stay in this miserable place? I could put the whole town in my hip pocket."

"You're comparing it with Guthrie," Grimes said in rebuke. "You can't put Ingalls up against Guthrie."

"I wouldn't put Ingalls up against anything," Chad said sourly.

Grimes drove down one street, then up another.

"If you're doing this for my benefit, you needn't bother." The sourness remained in Chad's voice. "In the first glimpse of it, I saw all of the town I wanted."

"I'm trying to see what facilities it has," Grimes replied. "We need a place to stay and a stable to put the team in. I'd like to spot a doctor too."

Chad had to wait until his coughing stopped before he could answer. "I told you this cough's nothing. I just got some dust in my lungs. It'll work out."

"If it doesn't kill you first," Grimes said dryly.

He clucked to the team and turned a corner. The wagon passed a sorry barn with big letters, "H. F. Pierce, Livery and Stable." Its big door was open and, as far as Grimes could see, there were no customers in the barn now.

"There's our livery stable," he said with satisfaction.

"It looks like it's going to fall down any minute," Chad said. "What kind of service can you get there?"

"You're still comparing Ingalls with Guthrie. That sets your standards too high for Ingalls."

"I don't have any standards at all for this hole in the ground. If this passes for a livery stable, what kind of accommodations are we going to find for ourselves?"

"Not the best, I'd say," Grimes said wryly. "We'll have to just do with what we find."

He turned at the next corner, drove a block, then said, "There's your accommodations."

Chad's eyes bulged with disbelief. He read the sign extending out from the second floor. "I wouldn't put hogs in that place."

"Get used to rooting around," Grimes chuckled. "If we can find accommodations, that's where we're going to stay."

Chad kept up a steady muttering as his brother halted the team beside the hotel. It started out as a two-story building. It had the height in front — there were even windows in that extra height — but the rest of the building tailed off sharply. It was one sorry-looking building. It probably had been from the time it was built. A big double door, flanked on both sides with long windows, marked the front. It was a frame building, sided with clapboards.

Once it had probably been white. Now, faded and dingy as it was, it was hard to say what its original color was.

"I can't believe it," Chad muttered as he climbed down from the wagon. He picked up a battered valise from the wagon's bed and followed Grimes toward the double doors. He stopped briefly before a huge cottonwood tree not more than twenty paces from the hotel. "Maybe we can camp out here under the tree," he said. "It'd be better than what we'll find inside."

Grimes laughed. Chad was still judging by Guthrie's standards, and poor Ingalls didn't have a chance.

He walked into the tiny lobby, Chad behind him. The lobby was in front of the hotel, and it had no more room than enough to hold a couple of dilapidated chairs. The upholstery was badly worn, tufts of stuffing showing in a dozen places. Chad almost choked as he looked at them. He wouldn't trust either of them to hold his weight. One of them was occupied by a frail-looking, thin old man, dozing peacefully. It would be all right for that old man. He didn't weigh what Chad did.

A small counter had been built across a corner, and a woman stood behind it. Her alert eyes watched every step they took across the small lobby.

"Howdy," Grimes said pleasantly. "I'm Frank Holloway. This is my brother, Chad. We heard there's some good land around Ingalls. We're here to see if we can find a good piece of it."

"Miss Ellsworth," she said, no emotion showing in her voice. "This is my hotel. Anything I can do for you?"

She didn't seem overly anxious to serve them, Chad thought dourly. If her manner was any indication of what they would find in this town, he didn't think they would have a very pleasant stay.

"This seems like a nice place," Grimes said jovially. Chad almost choked on the description. "We were hoping we could find accommodations here."

"How long do you plan on staying?" Miss Ellsworth asked.

Grimes shrugged. "That's hard to say. We want to do some looking around. It depends upon what we find. We may stay a week or more."

She eyed them in frank appraisal. Chad could almost swear there was hostility in those veiled eyes. "You should be able to find what you want in that time," she said. "You're fortunate. I've got just one room left. It's upstairs in the front. The window gives a nice view of the town."

Chad wanted to howl in indignation. That big cottonwood tree would effectively cut off any view. And who would want to give more than a casual glimpse to this town? Grimes was watching him, and Chad caught his small frown. He kept his lips clamped so no word could slip out.

"Sounds good to us," Grimes said heartily. "Could we see it?"

She didn't seem too pleased by the request, but she took a key down from a small collection and led the way upstairs. She opened the door and stepped aside to let them look at the room.

The room was worse than Chad had expected. It was barely big enough to hold a white, cast-iron bed. Some of the paint was flaking off. The only other item in the room was a weary-looking washstand, with a chipped bowl and pitcher on top of it.

"There's other facilities in back of the hotel," she said crisply.

Chad had reached the endurance of his patience. "You mean an outhouse?" he asked.

"What else did you expect?" she asked waspishly. She didn't seem to care whether or not they took the room.

Another furious glance from Grimes stopped

Chad's outbreak. "We'll take it, ma'am."

"It's two dollars a day. Payable in advance. Do you want to come back down and register?" She looked at Chad with scornful eyes. "You didn't expect a hotel like this would even have a register, did you?"

Chad looked at the floor and didn't answer. He could feel Grimes's resentful eyes on him.

The two followed her back to the desk, and Grimes signed the register. "I'll pay for ten days, ma'am. Could we take more if our business isn't finished here?"

"That can be arranged," she said coldly.

Grimes turned the dog-eared register so that Chad could sign. For an instant, Chad couldn't remember the name his brother had used, and he was frantic until his eyes caught Frank's bold handwriting. He was seething as he signed the false name under Frank's signature.

Grimes counted out two ten dollar bills and said, "Thank you, ma'am. We'll be back."

"You'd better take your key," she said crisply.

Grimes grinned. "I guess I should." He pocketed the key and walked out the door, Chad at his heels.

Chad held his temper until they reached the wagon. "This is the worst place I ever saw," he exploded. "Did you ever see a worse room?"

"It'll probably keep the rain off of you," Grimes replied. He was amused by the whole thing.

"I doubt that," Chad stormed. "Did you see that mattress? It looked lumpier than badly cooked oatmeal. We won't get a decent night's sleep on that thing. There wasn't even a blanket laid out on it."

"It's hot weather," Grimes said. "We won't need it. Are you forgetting why we came up here? I thought you were going to blow everything when you signed the register."

"I forgot the name you used until I looked at your signature. Why pay her twenty dollars? We won't be here that long."

"We might be here longer," Grimes replied. "Stop fuming over spending the money. I can bill Nix's office for it. Will you stop carping? Don't you want to do a job for Nix?"

Chad climbed into the wagon and looked back at the hotel as they drove away. "That's the most God-awful place I ever saw. And you're talking of spending more time in it. Why should Bill Doolin hang around a place like this town?"

"I'm getting damned tired of your belly-aching," Grimes said wearily. "It's an ideal place for an outlaw to pick. Out of the way, and no law. He can hide out without anybody being the wiser."

"Maybe," Chad said sullenly. "Where are you going now?"

"To find that doctor for your cough medicine."

"I told you I didn't need it," Chad said.

"Is that why you coughed three times while we were in that hotel?" Grimes asked sardonically.

"You going to bill Nix for the medicine, too?" Chad jeered.

"No," Grimes said calmly. "That's our expense. Also, the drugstore might be a good place to pick up some information. Doctors usually know what's going on in town. You never know when a lead will crop up."

Chad rode in sullen silence. Grimes drove down one street, then up another. Nobody could pay Chad enough money to get him to live here.

"Ah," Grimes said. "That might be our place." He pointed out a sign hanging from a small building. The sign read "Drugstore and Undertaking Parlor."

"What makes you think you'll find a doctor here?" Chad asked.

Grimes stopped the wagon, got out, and tied the team to the hitch rack. "If there isn't a doctor, we can get something for that cough.

When they first start out, doctors usually open up a drugstore and an undertaking business. It all seems to tie together."

"You know all the answers, don't you?" Chad asked in a grouchy tone. He followed Frank into the building. No sensible doctor would even think of starting a practice in a town like this; he'd wind up starving to death.

There was only one person in the store, and the sight of her stopped Chad short, stripping all the sullen unhappiness from his face. Girls were no novelty in his life, but one like this girl was. "Hello there," he said softly. When he wanted to turn on the charm, Chad could do it, and he put his best efforts into the attempt. The girl melted before the smile and the voice. "Hello," she returned. "Can I do something for you?"

Chad's eyes were devouring her. She was on the small side, but sweetly made. Her hair was a shining black. No, that was wrong. The sun streaming in the west window suddenly fastened on her hair. Chad changed his evaluation; her hair wasn't black at all. The sun picked out red highlights, and Chad almost wanted to purr with his delight. Her face was soft enough, but the chin was firm with a trace of toughness in it. Chad couldn't pick out a flaw in her features. The nose was a single clean stroke, and the lips were the rosiest, the softest he had ever looked at. He judged her to be about his age, maybe a year or two younger.

"I'm Chad Grimes," he said impulsively. He realized his slip and colored. Frank was glowering at him. "I mean Chad Holloway," Chad amended. "I've got an uncle named Chad Grimes. I was thinking of him." He was flustered, and he hoped it didn't show. God, he hoped she hadn't caught his slip. Frank's eyes were drilling through him.

For a moment, those lovely blue eyes were colder than ice, then they warmed. She extended a small hand. "I'm happy to meet you, Mr. Holloway." She blushed sweetly. "I'm Nella Ellsworth."

Chad sighed with relief. His slip hadn't stuck in her mind. But it sure had in Frank's mind, for that was pure murder in his eyes. "This is my brother, Frank Holloway." Chad got the name right this time, but it didn't lessen the disapproval in Frank's eyes.

To get his mind off of Frank's displeasure, he kept his attention focused on the girl. "We're looking for land around here. Say! Wouldn't that be fine if we wound up being neighbors?"

"I'd like that," she said softly.

Lord, Chad hadn't noticed those dimples

until she smiled again. She was the sweetest little thing he had ever looked at.

Grimes thought it time to break it up. "We came in to see if there's a doctor here. I want him to look at my brother. Chad has had a racking cough for too long."

"Dr. McMurty opened this drugstore, but he isn't here anymore." The girl seemed anxious to keep the conversation going.

"You mean he left town?" Grimes asked, frowning.

"More than that," she answered soberly. "He died." Before Grimes could look fully startled, she hastened to add, "But Dr. Swanson took his place. He's in the back room, attending to a corpse. He's also the town's only undertaker. Go right on back. He'll be glad to talk to you." An impish smile displayed those dimples again. "I'm sure your brother won't mind."

Grimes grinned as he nodded his thanks. He looked for the door of the back room, and glanced over his shoulder. "You coming, Chad?"

"Go ahead. I want to stay and talk a minute with Miss Ellsworth."

Grimes's scowl said he didn't appreciate that. It didn't bother Chad. It had been a long time since he had talked to a girl as cute as this one. Chad didn't intend to pass up the opportunity.

He waited until the door closed behind Grimes. "We just checked in at the O.K. Hotel, Miss Ellsworth. That's funny," he went on. "The landlady's name is the same as yours. Any relation? You sure don't look alike."

"We're not really related," she explained. "She's my stepsister. Her family adopted me when I was pretty young."

Chad caught the tiny frown line in her forehead. "I'm sorry," he said sincerely. "You look like it's been rough."

"Not really," she hastened to assure him. "Though sometimes Edith could be bossy. I worked for her at the hotel until I was lucky enough to get this job. This is better here. I get more opportunity to meet more interesting people."

"Imagine things could get boring in this little dump of a town."

Her eyes flashed. "It's not that bad. I've known some good times in Ingalls."

Chad saw that he had offended her, and he started to apologize. The back door opened, and Grimes stood in the doorway. "Chad," he called. The imperative tone left no doubt that he meant now.

"I gotta go now," Chad said hastily. "But I'll get a chance to see you again."

Her shrug said she didn't care one way or the other.

Chad was crestfallen as he walked to the door. He had talked too much. It was his one big failing.

"You could have waited a little longer," he complained. "I was just getting to know her."

"I imagine," Grimes said dryly. "Were you telling her all the details of your life?"

Chad's face flamed. "I was not," he said indignantly. "Do you think I've got a runaway tongue?"

"It ran away when you gave her your real name," Grimes pointed out.

"Ah, that was just a slip. I corrected it. She didn't even notice."

"You hope not," Grimes said bitingly. "Are you forgetting why we came up here? Another slip like that could cost you your life."

The sullen lines returned to Chad's face. "You're always fretting. I doubt that Doolin has even heard of Ingalls."

"Don't be so damned positive," Grimes snapped. He opened the rear door and pushed Chad ahead of him. "Wait until you see the corpse the doctor is working on."

Dr. Swanson was a man well up in his sixties. He was just preparing to put the lid back on the coffin. He looked up as Chad and

Grimes approached him, and he gave them a fleeting smile. "Always happy to get one of these jobs done," he said. His hair was snow white, and the veins were prominent in his hands.

"Doc, would you let Chad see who's in there?"

"Sure," Swanson said agreeably. "Though I'll never know why people want to look at a dead man. I've got him fixed up. You should have seen him when I was first called out to him." He slid off the lid and let it rest against the coffin.

Chad agreed with the doctor's sentiments about looking at dead people. He had seen only a few, and a lump always rose in his throat. His eyes rested briefly on the waxen face. A thin line of black moustache broke up the pallor of the face.

Chad started to look away, then the memory of a poster he had seen in Nix's office came back to him, and he forced himself to gaze fixedly at the corpse. He should know who this was, but no name came to him.

"Doc," Grimes said. "Can you put a name to him?"

"That's easy," Swanson answered. "That's Ol Yantis. Everybody around here knows him."

The information almost jarred unwise words

68

out of Chad. Grimes was waiting for just that, and he stopped Chad with a jerk of his head. "How come you're attending him?"

"Closest help the gang could find," Swanson replied. "Yantis was one of the Wild Bunch. He was tied up in a bank robbery in Spearsville, Kansas. They got a pretty good amount. I never did hear exactly how much. But the robbery put the law officers on their trail." Swanson was a garrulous old man, and his tongue wagged on.

Grimes tried to urge caution on him. "Doc, aren't you afraid the rest of the bunch will hear about your talking and try to shut you up?"

A ghost of a smile touched Swanson's lips. "All they could do is kill me. I never worry about that anymore. I'm an old man."

Grimes gave up. Talking was probably the only pleasure the old man had left. "Looks like the law officers ran him down."

"Yantis made it back to the hideout before the law caught up with him. The robbers split up. Yantis headed for his sister's home near Orlando. Deputies Marshal Madsen and Thomas Heuston and two others cornered him there. They called on Yantis to surrender. Yantis opened fire on the officers and was shot to pieces. I was called out. I saw there was nothing anybody could do for him. When I got to him, Yantis was bleeding hard. One bullet struck him in the right side and ranged downward, severing his spinal column. The officers questioned him about the robbery, but Yantis was tough to the last. He cursed the law officers and refused to talk. He was still cursing them when he died. I had him loaded in a wagon and hauled here."

Chad was breathing harder. "Do they know who the other robbers were?"

"Just guessed," Swanson replied. "They think it was Bill Doolin and Newcomb. It was reported that Doolin was shot in the foot. It could be so. He limps pretty badly."

"You've seen Doolin around here?" Grimes asked incredulously.

"Often," Swanson said laconically. "Around Ingalls, he goes and comes as he pleases."

There was furious accusation in Grimes's eyes as he looked at Chad. Chad mentally squirmed as he remembered stating that coming here was a wild goose chase, that they would find none of the Wild Bunch around Ingalls.

Swanson turned his head as the door opened. "Yes, Nella?" he asked.

Miss Ellsworth stood there, her eyes unreadable. But her face was white and frozen. She didn't look at all like the girl Chad

70

had left a few moments ago.

"Mrs. Dawson is after her prescription, Doctor. She seems impatient."

"They always are," Swanson said irritably. "Tell her I'll be out in a moment." He looked at Grimes. "You wanted to ask me about your brother's cough."

Chad felt a cough coming on, and he tried to stifle it. He failed. He coughed hard for a long moment, and his eyes were watering when he got it under control.

"Does it sound bad enough for him to do something about it?" Grimes asked.

"It does," Swanson said crisply. "Come with me. I think I have something that will help."

The three walked out of the room, and Nella was talking to a red-faced, plump woman. "Mrs. Dawson," Swanson said and nodded to her.

"Doctor," she said indignantly. "My prescription was supposed to be ready this morning. I've been back twice, and Nella says it still isn't ready."

Swanson's withdrawn expression showed that this woman was no favorite of his. "It's been a frantic day, Mrs. Dawson. I'll have it for you right away. But first I have to attend to these gentlemen. They were here before you."

He left her spluttering indignantly. He

71

peered near-sightedly at a row of bottles on a shelf. He selected one, its contents a poisonous-looking green. "I think this will do it. Take it every two hours for a couple of days. Come back and see me if it doesn't do any good."

Nella was busy, trying to placate Mrs. Dawson, and she wouldn't look at Chad as he passed her. Her lips were pressed in a tight, thin line as though she tasted something bad.

"What's wrong with her?" Grimes asked as they stepped outdoors.

"Damned if I know," Chad said miserably. "She wasn't like that when I first left her."

"Something must have happened," Grimes persisted. "Come on, Chad. Think of what it was."

"I'm trying to," Chad said, his face all screwed up in an effort to recall every word that had passed between them. "We were getting along good. We even exchanged names. I mentioned she had the same name as the woman who runs the O.K. Hotel. Nella said she lost her parents when she was young. The Ellsworth family adopted her. That was all. If that was enough to change her, I'm in the dark."

Grimes stopped short, his face savage. "You goddamned fool," he said passionately.

"You and your big mouth. You've already told her your real name. Why don't you yell it out to the entire town?"

Chad was round-eyed with bewilderment. "What did I do wrong?" he asked.

"We don't know how long she was at that door. She may have heard everything Swanson told us about Yantis and Doolin."

Chad blinked under this onslaught. "Are you saying she's going to take that information to that Ellsworth woman at the hotel? That's like saying there's some kind of connection between the woman and Doolin."

Grimes's outrage didn't lessen. "We don't know there isn't." He was silent for a few paces. "I think the smartest thing we can do is to get out of here as fast as we can. We've got the information we came to get." He cocked an eye at the darkening skies. "We can't leave tonight. I'm not too keen on driving these roads at night. We'll get back to the hotel and spend the night there. We can get an early start in the morning." He shivered as though a cold wind had suddenly enveloped him. "That can't come too soon to suit me."

Chad couldn't understand why terror had suddenly seized Frank. "What's chewing on you?"

"I just got a chill up and down my spine. I

don't know what connection those two women have with Bill Doolin, but I'd bet everything we have that in some way they'll get the news that two strangers are in town, talking about Yantis and Doolin. Don't you get it?" he asked in rising exasperation as the blankness didn't leave Chad's face. "Doolin will be damned curious as to why those strangers are showing so much interest in his Wild Bunch."

"If he's anywhere around here," Chad said skeptically.

"What does it take to pound some sense into your head?" Grimes cried. "He's here. Or somewhere near. You heard the doctor."

Chad was a stubborn man. "I didn't put too much stock in that old man. He had a loose tongue."

"Did he make up Yantis? You saw him in his coffin. Chad, you're too hard-headed for your own good."

His brother was deadly serious, and his manner washed over Chad. "You really think we could be in trouble."

"Not could be," Grimes corrected. "We are in trouble. I wish to God we had brought guns. But Nix didn't think that was too good an idea. Farmers usually don't go around carrying guns with them."

Chad was finally subdued by his brother's

grave manner. "What are we going to do?"

"Get back to that hotel room as fast as we can. If Doolin hears about this, and I'm betting he does, I don't think he'll break down the door to get at us. Maybe we can slip out early in the morning."

They left the wagon at the side of the hotel and walked into the hotel. The lobby was empty. Damn Frank and all his wild speculations. Chad had cold chills running up and down his spine too. He had fully expected to see that Miss Ellsworth standing in the lobby, balefully regarding them with ominous eyes.

Chad breathed easier as Grimes closed and locked the room door behind them. "We forgot something," Chad said suddenly.

"What's that?"

"We forgot to get something to eat. It's going to be a long night. My belly is already growling."

Grimes smiled bleakly. "That's the least of our worries. If your belly's too empty, take a long swig of your cough medicine. You're supposed to be taking it anyway."

Chad was muttering as he uncapped the bottle, tilted it up, and took a long swallow. His face was contorted as he swallowed. "That's the worst stuff I ever tasted. I don't know which is the worst: that damned medicine, or the fear that Doolin is coming."

Grimes sat down on the edge of the bed. "Just pray we don't find out." He looked out of the window. "Well, we can be thankful our room is on the second floor. You keep your ears open."

"Why?" Chad demanded.

"To listen for anybody trying to slink up the stairs."

Chad wasn't still fully convinced. Frank was letting the wildest of imaginations run away with him. He lay down on the other side of the bed, staring up at the darkening ceiling. He still couldn't believe what Frank thought about Nella. He remembered how those dimples had come and gone. She wasn't like that. He sighed dolorously — he had to admit that Grimes could be right. Damn, but this was going to be one long night.

CHAPTER 5

Nella was breathing hard as she reached the hotel. She had run all the way from the drugstore. She caught a long breath as she saw only Edith behind the counter in the lobby.

"You're off early," Edith Ellsworth said as Nella approached her. There was not a lot of love lost between the two women. They had been raised in the same family, but a natural animosity between them had never been fully throttled.

"I'm not off yet," Nella said. "Did the two strangers come back yet?"

Edith's eyes clouded over with suspicions. "What do you know about those two?"

"Not much," Nella replied. "But I don't think they're what they're pretending to be."

Edith's suspicions grew. Outside of Nella, no one in town knew that she had been secretly married to Bill Doolin for nearly two years now. She had thought Doolin was nothing more than a dashing cowboy with a zest for life. She had gone quietly to Kingfisher, where she became Mrs. William Doolin. His wounding stripped off the cloak he hid behind. A bullet had penetrated his left heel and torn along the arch to the ball of his foot, shattering the bone. Bill had been in considerable agony, and under that pressure had confessed what he had been doing. He had begged her to leave him, but he needed her more than ever. His charm and need fully captured her, and she wouldn't listen to him. Would it have made any difference if she had known what he actually was at the first? She had asked herself that question dozens of times and always came up with the same answer. She guessed not. He gave her more than an adequate life, and she loved him. What he did for a living didn't really matter to her. She guessed there was the same wild, reckless streak in her for she admired his daring and boldness. Doolin's money had bought this hotel for her, and she ran it with only one purpose in mind. She could keep her eyes open and let Doolin know when anybody suspicious stopped here. The country seemed to be crawling with marshals. They were being commissioned so fast Doolin couldn't keep up with them. She turned gladly to this new role, reporting any suspicious character who stopped at the hotel.

"Go on," Edith said impatiently.

"The strangers didn't notice me," Nella continued. "I listened to what Doctor Swanson told them. He said that was Ol Yantis in the coffin, then he told how Ol had been shot. He also said that he had seen Bill around Ingalls many times. Bill wasn't hard to recognize. Bill had been shot in the foot, and he still limped from the wound."

Edith's bosom rose and fell with the rapidity of her breathing. "They were lawmen. That old fool really marked Bill for them. Did they seem interested?"

"It stuck out all over them," Nella said passionately. That one called Chad was nothing but a liar, trying to deceive me, Nella thought. She didn't care what happened to him. "I thought you'd be interested," Nella finished.

Edith patted her hand. "You done good. I thought there was something fishy in those two's story. Always talking about the land they wanted to buy. All the time they were up here, they were trying to get a lead on Bill. I've got to get this news to Bill. Are you going to stay here until I get back? I won't be gone long."

Nella shook her head. "I can't. I'm not off

work yet. I told the doctor I had to run an errand. I've got to get back."

Edith nodded. "Bill will appreciate this, Nella. It'll stop some damned law officer from trying to ambush him." She felt a surge of gratitude. They had never really gotten along before. Their natures were so diverse that they had quarreled many times. For the moment, all that was gone.

She watched Nella walk out of the hotel, and her mind jumped in several directions at once. She didn't know where the two strangers were. If they had come in, she had been too busy to notice them. But this information was vital to Bill. A sob welled up in her throat. She didn't know where Bill was. She wiped away the weakness with an iron hand. Losing her head now wasn't going to do Bill or herself any good. She forced herself to think rationally. She would look in Ransom's Saloon first. Bill spent a great deal of time there.

The sun was down as she left the hotel, but the heat hadn't abated. The coming darkness put a new terror in Edith. All she could think of was the flame of gunfire stabbing out of the darkness and Bill falling. She knew the marshals would shoot Bill down without giving him any preliminary warning. She hurried her pace until she was almost running.

She was breathing hard as she entered the place. Four customers were in the room, and none of them belonged to Bill's bunch. Murray frowned as she came in. Women rarely came into this place, and he didn't want to break that tradition. His face cleared as he recognized Edith. That was Doolin's woman. Doolin would skin him alive if he didn't give her every consideration.

Edith walked to the far end of the bar and beckoned to him. All male eyes had swung curiously to her, wondering why she was in here. She didn't want any of them to overhear her real purpose.

Murray hurried down the bar. "What is it, Edith?"

"Do you know where Bill is? I've got to talk to him." Her words came faster. She had to make him realize how important her visit was. "It could be vital to Bill, Murray."

"Why, he's in the back room," he said. What was important to a woman wasn't always important to a man. They could build up anything all out of proportion.

She guessed what was in his mind and smiled bleakly at him. She didn't give a damn what he thought as long as she found Bill.

She opened the door to the rear room, where a poker game was in progress. The air was thick with cigarette and cigar smoke. She heard a rich string of oaths as a player tossed away a losing hand. The profanity didn't bother her. She had heard everything any of these men could say.

"Bill," she called. "I've got to see you."

He turned his head and looked at her. The momentary annoyance vanished. He didn't question her reasons; he just stood and limped over to her.

"What's bothering you, honey?" he drawled.

In a hushed voice, she related everything Nella had told her. He didn't argue or look skeptically at her; he just listened, his face growing tighter with every word.

"Sounds like the good doctor is talking too much for his own good," he said lazily.

She clutched his arm, and her fingers were frantic. It wasn't the doctor she was worried about; it was the two strangers in town. "Bill, what about the two strangers? They could be marshals."

He patted her hand and smiled. "Don't you fret your pretty head, honey. Did those two strangers come back to the hotel?"

"I don't know," she said miserably.

"But they will," he assured her. "They've got to have a place to sleep." His eyes narrowed as he thought. "What room did you give those two?"

"An upstairs front room. The one opposite the big tree in front."

"I remember that tree." His eyes had a savage glint. "Don't worry anymore about it. I'll take care of everything. You just get on back and act as though nothing's happened." He brushed her forehead lightly with his lips. "You done real good, baby." He turned her and gently shoved her toward the door. "Go on, now. I'll need somebody to report if those two go out, won't I?"

She nodded, all her fears suddenly quieted. Bill would know exactly what to do in this emergency.

Bill waited until the door closed behind her, then limped back to the table. "Game's over," he announced.

Waightman looked up at the arresting note in Bill's voice. "Something up?"

"Could be," Doolin drawled. "Edith told me something interesting. There's two strangers in town. They claim they're interested in buying some farmland."

"But you think there's something more," Waightman said.

"I know there is," Doolin said firmly. He told the listening men about the visit to Swanson's drugstore. "They were too damned interested in Yantis. Swanson spilled his guts. He told them all about me, and even told them how I limped about. That might've been just idle talk, or it could be something far more important. In any case, I think the good doctor has talked too much. Red, take care of him."

Waightman nodded, his eyes glinting savagely. "Never did trust that old fool," he rumbled.

Doolin nodded and waited until he left the room. He turned to the other three. "Edith says the two strangers took an upstairs room — the one just opposite that big ol' tree. If a man could climb that tree, it would give him an open shot at that room."

Heads bobbed in appreciation. Bill had the answer to every problem that faced him.

"Who wants the job?" Doolin asked.

Tulsa Jack reached down and picked his Winchester from the floor beside his chair. "Why, that sounds like a job that fits me."

"Think you can climb that tree?" Doolin asked.

Jack grinned. "Can a squirrel climb?"

Doolin clapped him on the shoulder. "Take care of it. We can't afford to have the peace of Ingalls disturbed by noisy strangers."

CHAPTER 6

"What time is it now?" Chad asked.

Grimes cussed as he tugged the big silver watch from his pants pocket. There was barely enough light left in the room for him to make out the figures. "You asked me that not ten minutes ago," he said crossly. "It's seven-thirty."

"Is that all?" said Chad unhappily. He stood and walked the length of the room. Three paces one way and three paces back. He looked like a caged animal.

"That's not going to do you any good," Grimes said. "It won't make the time pass any quicker. Why don't you lie down and try to get to sleep."

"I tried that," Chad growled. "Sleep wouldn't come." He was in the midst of turning, and he jerked as he heard a sharp, cracking noise. "I thought I heard a shot," he remarked.

"You did," Grimes said calmly. "That was probably a rifle shot."

"Right in town?" Chad asked.

"Maybe somebody wanted to scare away a coyote that came too close to town," Grimes said.

"You don't believe that," Chad said.

"No, I don't," Grimes confessed. "But that's not the first shot this town's heard. It won't be the last either."

"You think somebody got hit?" Chad asked in a subdued tone.

"I wouldn't be surprised," Grimes said. "And quit speculating who it was. That won't do you any good."

Chad's voice rose. "Jesus Christ! Are we going to have to spend the night here?"

The dryness remained in Grimes's voice. "It's a lot safer than being down there on the street. Or do you want to try that?"

"We could try to slip out of town under the cover of darkness," Chad suggested.

"No! I'd rather wait until dawn, then try to slip out. Fewer people will be up and about."

"Do you think Doolin could be looking for us?" Chad's restless pacing started again, three paces one way, turn, and three paces back.

Grimes didn't know how much longer he

could stand Chad's restlessness. He managed to control his voice. "I wouldn't be at all surprised," he said flatly. The girl in the drugstore had overheard Swanson. She was related to the woman who ran this hotel. Chad had said the girl changed a lot. Maybe she had reported the talk to someone far more deadly. The room was suddenly stifling, and when he touched his forehead he wasn't surprised to find his fingertips wet. God, this could be a spot but, as he had pointed out to Chad, there wasn't a damned thing they could do about it. This was about as safe a spot as they could find in Ingalls. He'd be really sweating if they had a first-floor room. That would make them that much more readily accessible. He didn't blame Chad for feeling tight. Grimes had the same feeling. If only Nix hadn't insisted they take no guns. It might tear their cover wide open, but they wouldn't feel so naked.

The room was almost dark now and Chad said petulantly, "Can't we turn on the lamp?"

"What do you want to do, make the target easier for somebody?" Grimes snapped. "We sit in the darkness." He thought of something and stood. The blind was up. Drawing it wouldn't furnish any protection except that it might cut off inquisitive eyes.

He walked around the bed and approached

the window. He stopped abruptly. "You hear anything, Chad?"

Chad listened a moment. "I don't hear anything."

Grimes sighed. The noise he heard was probably the scrambling of an animal in the tree. It wouldn't be a squirrel at this hour. But the darkness wouldn't prevent a cat from clawing its way up the tree.

He continued on to the window and hesitated before he lowered the blind. Maybe he could spot what had made that sound.

He stared out of the window and saw nothing. "I'm imagining things, Chad." He started to add something more and never had the opportunity.

A flash of flame lanced out of the tree, dazzlingly brilliant for a moment. Grimes didn't hear the report of the shot. All he knew was the shocking jolt of the bullet. He tried to cry out, and his mouth wouldn't work. He half whirled, then fell heavily.

Chad sprang toward the window. "What the hell?" he started. He never finished the sentence. Again, the tongue of fire reached out from the tree, and Chad knew nothing more as everything was blotted out for him.

Tulsa Jack was whistling as he walked into

Ransom's Saloon. He had the warm, comfortable feeling of a man doing his job thoroughly and well. "Bill still here, Murray?"

Murray nodded. "He's still back there." He jerked his head toward the rear room.

Jack walked into the room and sprawled out in a chair. He reached for a bottle and filled a glass. He raised the glass and gulped down its contents.

"Well?" Doolin asked impatiently.

Jack grinned. "Simple. I saw both of them fall."

"Do you think you got them?"

"Would I be back here if I hadn't?" Jack's indignation rose. He didn't like to be questioned about the quality of his work. "Did you ever know me to miss?"

Doolin stood and walked over to stop behind Jack's chair. He clapped him on the shoulder. "I never did," he admitted. It was small wonder he was so successful, picking men like this. Just as added insurance, he would have Edith check the room and report on the bodies. "Maybe this will teach Nix to quit sending his damned marshals up here."

Jack laughed in uproarious delight. "Maybe he's getting it through his thick head that Ingalls belongs to you."

CHAPTER 7

Chad fought returning to consciousness. He had an instinctive knowledge that told him it would mean returning to a world of pain and suffering. He cautiously opened his eyes and looked about the darkened room. He was lying on the floor, and for a moment couldn't quite place where he was. Then it all came back to him with a rush, and that opened the floodgates to pain. It felt as though his head was coming off, and he ground his teeth against the ache. Awareness came filtering back slowly. He had been shot when he approached that window. How vividly he remembered that stabbing lance of flame that reached out of him, the momentary feeling that his head was splitting open, then the blackness. He wished he hadn't had to leave that blackness. It was all so peaceful, and he hadn't hurt.

A persistent sound kept picking at him, and for a moment, he couldn't place what it was. Then the knowledge hit him with a crushing weight. That was Frank making that distressed sound. Frank had been shot first; Chad had seen him go down. He had tried to reach Frank, and the second shot had dropped him. He lay there a moment longer, listening to Frank's wheezing, agonizing breathing. He had to do something about that; he had to get to Frank. For a long moment, the effort of making the attempt seemed too much, then he tried. He got his arms under him and raised his torso. My God! He didn't realize he was so weak. He wanted to sag back to the floor, but he forced his weak arms to support his weight. He hung there for an eternity, his head drooping toward the floor. Just that little effort made it feel as though his head was coming apart. He stayed in that position until the pounding eased in his head and he could think again. He raised himself to a sitting position, and he was breathing hard when he was half upright. His head felt as though some evil, lusty blacksmith was using it for an anvil. The hammer was attuned with each breath, and just as sure as that breath came, so would the pounding of the hammer.

That was odd. There seemed to be an echo of

his breathing for, in between breaths, he heard that labored wheezing. That was Frank! He had been going to him when the effort he put out nearly blacked him out. Before he moved again, he touched his head, hoping to somehow lessen that murderous aching. He felt a shallow gash just above his right ear, and it felt sticky. His fingers continued gingerly exploring. The blood had flowed down his right cheek, and he could feel the stiff caking of it there. He had done quite a bit of bleeding, but apparently it had almost stopped. He was fortunate that he had been standing where he was. Just a fraction of an inch to the left, and he would have been a dead man. He heard that wheezing breathing again, and it seemed to carry a frantic pleading in it.

Chad dropped to his hands and knees and crawled the few feet between him and Frank. That damned blacksmith was back to work again. Chad tried to ignore his jolting strokes.

He found Frank by touch; his vision wasn't all it should be. "Frank, Frank," he begged. "How bad are you?"

For a long moment, he thought Frank was incapable of answering; then the slow, labored words came. "Pretty bad, Chad. Oh God, I thought you were a dead man. For a while, I could see you lying over there, but now my vision is thickening up."

"I'm fine, Frank," Chad tried to assure him. He didn't want the burden of him being wounded on Frank's mind. "What can I do for you?"

Frank's voice had grown so faint that Chad could barely hear it. "Nothing, Chad. I caught it. That noise I thought I heard out there was some bastard. . . ." He had to pause every few words to get enough strength to go on, "– climbing that tree to get a clear shot at us." His sigh was long and broken. "And I thought we would have a little safety here. I never figured on them climbing that tree. They're thorough, aren't they? I've been wrong all the way, Chad."

"Don't try to talk anymore," Chad begged. "I'll go and get a doctor. You'll be just fine –"

Frank interrupted him. "Stop talking like a kid, Chad." His voice grew fainter, and Chad had to put his ear close to his mouth to be able to catch the quavering words. "No doctor's going to do me any good. A man knows when he's had it. Besides, I don't want you out on those streets. That'd give them a clear shot at you. Get out of this room as fast as you can. I think I saw a back stairs. Get out before somebody comes to check on how successful they were."

Anguish was a cruel hand squeezing Chad's heart. "I can't leave you, Frank. I've got to stay —" His words were chopped off as Frank's head slumped to a shoulder.

Chad knew he was gone. He could tell by the sudden chill that seized his heart. But he tried a moment longer. He begged Frank to answer him, and there was only that dreadful silence. He sat there, trying to regroup his thoughts. He couldn't leave Frank, even though Frank insisted that he do so. Slowly, his thoughts grew more rational. Frank was right when he told him to try and get away. He couldn't do anything for Frank; nobody could.

Chad wasn't crying as he struggled to his feet, but he felt as though he was. His eyes were dry, but they stung, and his throat was so tight that it was a physical ache. He glanced about the room. There was nothing he needed to take with him. Yes, there was. He could take his hat. But first he wanted to wash the gash and blood-stained cheek. There was a little water in the pitcher, and he poured it out into the bowl. He doused the water on his cheek with an open hand, gritting his teeth as the sting of the water mounted. But that passed in a moment. He dried his face on a husk towel, reached for his hat and set it on the left side of his head to keep it from touching the wound.

He looked around the room again, his eyes resting longest on his brother. "I'm sorry, Frank," he whispered. "Maybe I can make this up to you." Right now, he didn't know how. Frank always had a great pride in everything he did. He wouldn't know that pride now; he hadn't finished this job for Nix. But maybe Chad could get to Nix and pass on the information that had cost Frank so dearly.

Chad eased out of the door, closing it softly behind him. He locked it, though that wouldn't do any good. Miss Ellsworth would have another key. "Damned bitch," he muttered. He had no doubt that somehow she was involved in this. That meant the girl Nella had a part also. "Another damned bitch," he growled under his breath.

There were steps at the rear of the hotel and, in the darkness, Chad felt his way down them. He thought his outstretched hands would never find the door that should be back here, but finally his fingers traced the long crack in one side of the door, then the door knob. He opened it with all the caution he could, and his heart jumped as the door squealed noisily. He cursed the door with a mental oath, opened the door only wide enough to slip through it, then left it standing ajar, not wanting to risk it squealing again.

He made his way around the hotel to the side where Frank had left the wagon. His stomach dropped out of him, leaving only a void, when he saw nothing there.

It took him a long moment to recover from the shock, then he was thinking again. The bastards had taken the team and wagon. Now there was no way of getting out of this miserable town unless he walked.

By God, he would walk all the way to Guthrie, if necessary. Nix had to know what he and Frank had discovered. He made his way to the rear of the hotel. From now on, he would have to keep to the backyards until he was out of town. He thought of the outhouse back here, and a grim humor touched him. He could sit there for a moment until the weakness in his legs faded. It sounded like a hell of a place to hide, but it might have an advantage at that. That would be the last place anybody would think of to look for him.

He had almost reached the outhouse when he froze as a voice said, "Hold it there, mister. Right where you are."

Chad thought he would collapse under the sheer fright the voice put into him. But wait a moment! That wasn't a man's voice; that was a woman speaking.

He turned slowly and faced Miss Ellsworth.

She held a pistol on him, and her face was tense.

"Why the gun?" He feigned surprise. "I was just going to the outhouse."

"You're a liar, mister," she said flatly. "You came around the hotel. What are you doing out of your room?"

He tried to sound amused. "Am I supposed to get permission to leave it?"

"Don't get smart with me," she said, hatred showing in her tone. "You were trying to leave Ingalls. You're coming with me."

"You're not the law," he protested.

"All the law I need," she said calmly.

Chad stiffened. How good was she with that gun? Could he cover the distance between them before she could pull the trigger?

She guessed at his thoughts. "Don't try anything," she said. "I've used this before."

If she wasn't competent, she sounded so. Chad forced himself to relax. "Where are you taking me?"

"To somebody who's got a lot of interest in you," she replied. "Bill will want to know all about you. He'll be interested why you're out of your room."

Chad swallowed hard. "You mean Bill Doolin?"

Again, he caught that mocking flash of her

teeth. "You guessed right, mister. Now turn around."

I failed you, Frank, he thought. I'm not going to get out of Ingalls. Doolin will see to that. Again, he evaluated his chances. It wouldn't be much difference being shot by her than by Doolin or one of his bunch. He knew what they would do.

He was still held by indecision when another voice said, "He isn't going anyplace, Edith."

Chad saw Nella just stepping around the corner of the hotel. She held a cavalry pistol, and the gun looked ridiculously big in her small hand. "Drop that gun, Edith." She made a small gesture with the pistol. "You know I can use this. You've seen me shoot before."

Rage twisted Edith's face as she struggled with this new dilemma. "Nella, you couldn't turn against Bill. You'll be sorry if he finds out."

That could have been a small sob rattling in her throat. "He won't find out."

"You couldn't turn against Bill. This man came up here to spy on him. Don't you remember everything Bill has done for you?"

"I remember," Nella said, and she struggled to keep back her tears. "He also shot Dr. Swanson just a short while ago. Or it was done by Waightman, one of his bunch. I saw Waightman across the street just before Dr. Swanson stepped out of his store. Shortly after that, the doctor was gunned down. That old man was good to me. He gave me a tremendous lift when I needed it."

"Haven't you forgotten how good Bill has been to you?" Edith's voice was sharp. "Dr. Swanson talked too much. He was dangerous to Bill."

Nella's lower lip quivered. "He didn't have to order the doctor killed. Edith, I'm not going to tell you again. Drop that gun."

Edith hesitated, and Nella snapped. "I mean it. Will it take a bullethole to convince you I meant what I said?"

Edith stared at her; then slowly her hand opened, and the gun fell to the ground. "I think you're crazy," she whispered.

Nella advanced slowly toward her, the gun never wavering. "Maybe I'm just sick of all the killing."

"Bill will never forgive you for this," Edith said in a vicious voice. "He'll run you down —"

"Turn around," Nella interrupted. "Damn it." Her voice grew shriller. "How many times do I have to tell you something?"

Edith turned her back on Nella, and Nella's hand holding the gun rose and fell. She struck with the barrel at the base of Edith's skull.

Edith groaned hollowly, and her legs turned to string, dumping her on the ground.

"My God," Chad said. "If I hadn't seen this, I wouldn't have believed it."

"Believe it," Nella snapped. "Do you want to get away from Ingalls, or are you just going to stand there?"

Chad shook his head. "There's no way for me to leave. They took my team and wagon."

She nodded. "I know. I saw it. I've got a horse tied just a short way off. I didn't dare bring it any closer to the hotel."

Chad could have whooped with his elation. "You can't stay here."

Her nod was weary. "I know. I could only get one horse. I'm leaving with you."

The picture of Frank lying dead and abandoned in that hotel room flashed before Chad's eyes. "I want to tell you something first. My brother was killed because of you."

She briefly closed her eyes. "I know," she said. Resentment firmed her face, and she snapped at him. "Damn you. Can't you see that I'm trying to make up for my mistake? I have no place else to go."

She looked such a pathetic figure, standing there with shoulders slumping. Pity weakened his dislike. She was trying to atone for her talking to Edith. "Come on," he said gruffly. "Where's that horse?"

Hope transformed her face. She handed him the gun. "Maybe you'd better take this."

Chad tucked the pistol in his waistband. The picture of her standing there holding that over-sized pistol came back to him, and he chuckled. "Would you really have shot her?"

"I don't know," she confessed. "But she thought I would."

"She sure did," Chad said. "Lead the way." His resentment of her was still with him. It was her responsibility that Frank was dead, but maybe there were extenuating circumstances in her favor. He would have to give that consider-able thought. He let her lead the way and hurried after her.

CHAPTER 8

Nella had the horse tied a good block away. "I didn't dare bring it any closer to the hotel. Somebody might see it and. . . ." A shudder finished the sentence.

"You did just fine," Chad said. He felt like hell. His head ached intolerably, and his legs trembled. Just the short walk had taken its toll. He wouldn't have been able to go much farther. He eyed the horse appreciably. "You picked out a good one."

She read something wrong in the words. "It belongs to me. I didn't steal it, if that's what you're inferring."

It was a strain to put the grin back on his face. Lord, this little one had a temper. It flashed out at the slightest provocation. "I didn't say you did," he said stiffly. He stopped and listened. The tension of the night was still with him. Every small sound, even the most ordinary one, had a new menace to it. He didn't know how large a margin of time they were working on, but it couldn't be much. Someone would find the unconscious woman, and after she was revived she would tell them what had happened. Doolin would send somebody after them, trying to cut them off. Nella was dead right when she remarked that she could no longer stay in Ingalls.

"Take the saddle," she urged. "I'll ride behind you."

He nodded and, in mounting, turned his head so that she caught a quick glimpse of his right cheek. There must have been traces of blood on it for she gasped. "You've been wounded."

"Nothing important," he said. "I'm all right." It brought back the hotel room, and his face and voice turned bleak. "Your Doolin did this to me." Yes, he thought. And killed Frank.

"I didn't know it would turn out like this," she said faintly. "He's more vicious or more desperate than I knew."

He climbed into the saddle and reached down a hand for her. She was as light as a feather, and he easily hoisted her up behind him. Her arms wrapped about his waist, and he felt the warmth of her body as she pressed against him. He noticed the canteen fastened to the horn and said, "You thought of everything."

"Not everything," she said with wry humor. "I didn't bring another horse, and I didn't include a rifle. I didn't dare walk around with one, even if I knew where to locate one."

"A rifle would have been fine," he said calmly. "We'll make it. Don't go blaming yourself for anything."

"But I do," she wailed. "I started all this by talking to Edith. I felt I owed it to her."

Chad put the horse into a slow walk. He wouldn't dare increase the speed until he thought they were safely out of town. "And she carried the information to Doolin?"

"Yes," she said weakly.

He thought about it a moment, then said, "Everything's started by somebody. None of this would have happened if Frank and I hadn't come to Ingalls." He could carry the thought a little further; Nix had really started it when he assigned them to look over Ingalls. It really went further back than that. He could blame the weather for helping them lose the farm. He could blame the banker for refusing to listen to Frank's pleas for help. Lord, a man could drive himself crazy trying to figure where the blame for anything really started.

He skirted the houses and buildings when he could avoid them. God, he would have given anything to put the horse into a full run, but a running horse drew attention quicker than anything else. "You didn't really know that Doolin is a wanted outlaw?"

"I swear I didn't," she breathed. "I knew there was a wild streak in him, but he was Edith's man. I guess I saw only what I wanted to see."

Chad pondered over what she said. It could be so. Hadn't she tried to atone by what she did? Chad tried to wash everything out of his mind. His judgment wasn't going to change what had happened.

He drew a breath of relief as he passed the last structure in Ingalls. Maybe he couldn't exult yet, but it looked as though they had made it. It was safe to let out the horse some.

He set the horse into a lope, and its even stride ate up the distance. "Keep an eye behind you," he advised Nella. "Let me know if you see anything."

He knew she was turning her head; he could tell by the way she loosened a hand on him.

"I don't see anything, Chad."

"Maybe we're luckier than we deserve," he muttered. He lifted the reins for more pace.

"How far do you plan on going?" Nella asked.

"Guthrie," he said brusquely. Right now, that seemed a formidable distance, but he wouldn't feel thoroughly safe until he was in Nix's office.

"Just keep watching," he said. Maybe they'd had too much luck. He frowned. Surely Doolin had discovered what had happened to Edith. When that came all hell would break loose. He could expect pursuit then. Don't flog your streak of luck, he thought. He couldn't push this horse too hard. Guthrie would be a brutal ride on an animal as doubly burdened as this one was.

He caught the first break in the rhythm of the horse's stride. At first, it was barely discernible, but it happened again. The horse was going lame.

Nella noticed the stiffening of Chad's figure. "Do you see something?" she asked, dread changing her voice.

"Not what you're thinking," he answered. "But we may be in trouble. I think your horse is going lame." He pulled up and said, "I'll have to check."

He slipped out of the saddle and helped her down. "I think he's favoring the right foreleg," he said. He handed her the reins to hold and raised the front hoof, murmuring as he did, "Easy, boy. Easy."

There was trouble in that leg, for the horse flinched and tried to jerk the leg away. "Easy, boy," he said more sharply. "Easy."

He lifted the hoof off the ground, and even in the darkness he found the trouble. A fair-sized stone had lodged in the frog, the tender part of the hoof.

Nella hung over him, her anxiety showing. "What is it, Chad?"

"He's picked up a stone," he said tersely. "Give me room."

He pulled a knife from his pocket and opened a blade. The light wasn't good, and he had to let his fingers locate the trouble. His fingers outlined the shape and position of the stone, and Chad got the point of the blade under the stone. He pried at it and set his teeth at its resistance. He would have to use more force and risk snapping off the blade. He pried harder, and the stone came free and dropped into his hand. He showed it to Nella and said, "There it is. A damned small thing to cause so much trouble."

She nodded, her face tight. "Will he be permanently lame?"

Chad shook his head. "I don't think so. I believe a rest will do him all the good in the world. But we better hadn't try to ride him for a while."

He saw her look toward Ingalls and knew what she was thinking. The thought bulked large in his mind. He was afraid that he would see or hear pursuit.

"The old Cutter place is just ahead," she said. At his frown, she added, "It's been deserted for a long time. It's in falling-down shape, but it might do for shelter until the morning."

"Worth a try," Chad agreed. He led the horse, and Nella trudged along beside him. Lord, what a small space of time could do to a person's condition. Less than an hour ago, she had been safe and secure in Ingalls. Now, she was a fugitive. He grinned fleetingly as he realized he was in no better shape himself. When a person got in a hole like this there was no map, no prior experience to use as a guide. He had to go ahead, almost blindly, and pray that everything turned out all right.

The old Cutter place loomed up before them about a hundred yards off the road. Chad wished that it were set much farther off the road, but beggars couldn't be choosers. He led the horse clear around the wreck of a house, where a lean-to in the rear must have served as an animal shelter. It too looked as though it was ready to fall down, but it would do to hold the horse. Chad led it inside, and stripped off saddle and bridle. He wished there were some hay or oats he could feed it. By God, he was full of wishes tonight, and not a single one was doing him any good.

He found a couple of loose boards and barricaded the door. It was a flimsy obstruction at best but lame as it was, he didn't think the horse would wander off.

He entered the old house first, flailing his arms to remove the cobwebs at the door. "All right, now," he called back. It was a sorry mess. Man worked so hard to build something, and it wound up like this. Most of the windows were out. Chad imagined passing kids had demolished them with well-flung rocks. A windowpane was an irresistible target for any boy. The roof was in sad repair. Through rents in it, Chad could see the sky overhead.

Dust was thick on the rotting floor, and Chad thought he could discern tiny tracks of mice and rats. It had been inhabited by small animals, but no man had entered the building for a long time.

"How long has it been deserted?" he asked.

"The last Cutter died when I was just a child," Nella replied. "Evidently, there was nobody to inherit or want it. It's sat out here for years, slowly rotting away." A shiver ran through her. "It's kinda spooky."

"It ain't much," Chad agreed with her. "But I'd rather have it than walking along the road. We sure can't ride the horse until at least in the morning. Maybe not even then," he finished gloomily. He tried to brighten his outlook. "There's no use moaning about it. Do you think the Wild Bunch knows about this place?"

There was enough light for him to make out Nella's forehead wrinkled in thought. "I honestly don't know," she confessed.

"Well, we'll just pray they don't. I wish this place set farther off the road. It can be seen by anybody passing along." He managed a grin for her. "We can't do much about that either."

He used his hat and fanned vigorously with it at the dust on the floor. He cleared a small space for her to sit down and coughed against the dust he raised.

"Damn it," he said plaintively. "That set my head to pounding."

She patted the floor beside her. "Sit down here and let me look at that wound." She made a brief examination of the shallow gash. "It doesn't look too bad." A note of dismay filled her voice. "I haven't anything to put on it." Her voice brightened. "I did bring the canteen in. Maybe I can wash it off."

"Good," he said in approval. She was using her head to think of bringing the canteen into the house.

She pulled a handkerchief from her pocket, poured water on it, and gently dabbed at the wound.

Chad kept his teeth clenched. That stung like hell.

"It looks better," she said as she finished.

"Stung some," he admitted. He moved over to a wall so that he would have something at his back. He looked at the empty eyes of the broken windows. "Good thing it's summer and not winter. We'd have some trouble keeping warm."

"Yes," she said, and laughed in a shaky voice. "Chad, I keep thinking of your brother and the part I had in it."

"Stop it," he said roughly. "You didn't deliberately plan on it happening that way, did you?" At the shake of her head, he went on, "Then nobody can blame you." He stopped and straightened.

"What is it?" she asked, instant alarm in her voice.

"I thought I heard something going by on the road." He crawled to a window and peered. "I did. Five horsemen." That didn't augur too well for them.

"What are they doing?" she asked breathlessly.

Maybe it was only a guess, but he thought she knew who the horsemen were. Chad had the same miserable guess as to their identity. It probably was Doolin and some of his bunch, looking for some trace of them.

"Ah," he said, finding a small relief. "They're moving on. They didn't even glance at this place."

"What should we do?" she asked. "Stay here, or move on?"

"We wouldn't get very far," he said with brutal candor. "Not with a lame horse. No, we'll wait it out and see what happens."

He watched the horsemen until they were out of sight. They couldn't have missed seeing the old house. It was funny they didn't investigate it further.

He crawled back to her. He didn't feel right about the incident. Doolin didn't have a reputation for carelessness. Chad's mind kept picking at the facts. Had Doolin seen horse tracks? If so, those tracks had turned off here. Why hadn't he looked further?

"Something's bothering you," she accused him.

"Yes," he admitted. "I just wish to hell I knew what they were doing."

He squirmed at the predicament they were in, caught in a flimsy old house that would afford no protection. If that bunch turned and came back, he and Nella were caught like rats in a trap. Was Doolin just checking to see that the horse tracks went no farther? Chad was trying to put himself in Doolin's place to figure out Doolin's next move.

He straightened and tensed as he heard the thud of hooves from a running horse. A running horse meant bad news, particularly in this region — more particularly so when it turned down the lane toward the house. A thought flashed into his mind, filling him with terror. The thought was not beyond the realm of possibility: not with Doolin behind it.

She sensed his fear and whispered, "What is it?"

He reached for her hand. "Come on. Get out of here. Don't ask any questions."

The tone of his voice effectively stopped her from speaking. He guided her to a rear window. "Hurry! Get out of here."

She seemed so slow, and Chad could wait no longer. There was no glass in the window, and he literally shoved her through it. He heard her indignant gasp as he dove through it, landing on one shoulder. He came to a stop and scrambled to his feet. He seized her hand again and said, "Move!" The thud of hooves was very close.

He drove for a skimpy bunch of trees, reaching it before the galloping horse reached the house. He dove into the trees and pulled her off her feet. "Get down!" he barked. "And stay there."

He could tell by her spluttering how indignant she was, but she offered no other protest. He squirmed his way to the most sizable tree, hoping it was big enough to furnish adequate protection. His fingers squeezed her arm, holding her there.

Maybe he was all wrong in his expectations. Now the hoofbeats seemed to recede.

He couldn't tell how much time passed, but it seemed an eternity. It couldn't have been more than a few seconds.

The explosion seemed close enough to shatter his eardrums. The house disintegrated before his eyes. The force of the explosion literally blew it to pieces, and it collapsed. His hearing had barely returned before a fire broke out in the debris.

She stared at what had once been a house with horror-filled eyes. She retained a grip on herself enough to keep her voice low. "What was that?" He felt her breath against his ear.

"I'd say a stick of dynamite," he whispered in

return. "The thought hit me when I heard that running horse. It'd be quick and thorough. Somehow, that bunch knew we were in there."

He could feel her shaking now. "Why, that's monstrous." He could barely hear her.

"Do you know of a better way to get rid of somebody you want eliminated?"

She started to rise, and he held her against the ground. "We're not sure they're gone."

The fire burned fiercely against the age-old boards.

"My horse?" she whispered, and she was indignant.

"We can't do anything about that now," he whispered back. "Ah," he murmured. "I thought they'd be showing up. Don't even breathe." He didn't hear a sound from her, but he could sense her pressing tighter against the ground.

Five men rode up and dismounted. They couldn't get too close to the fire because of the heat. Firelight reflected ruddily on their faces, and Chad recognized several of them from the pictures Nix had shown him. Doolin was there.

"I think that got them," Waightman said.

"A stick of dynamite usually does," Doolin replied dryly. "Still, I'd like to see the bodies just to be sure."

"No chance," Waightman said. "That dynamite blew them to hell."

"Poor Nella," Doolin said. "She was a nice kid, but she didn't know which side to stay on. Move around where the house stood and see if there's anything to see."

Chad's hand was against her back, and he pressed her more firmly against the ground. She didn't have to be told how vital silence was to them.

"There was a lean-to against the house," Tulsa Jack said. "I didn't know that."

"Lots of things you don't know," Waightman said. "If you want proof, Bill, there it is. That's the rear leg of a horse, and he wasn't as close to the explosion as those two were. Satisfied?"

"I am, now. Let's get the hell out of here. If that explosion doesn't pull somebody out here, the fire will. I don't want to be seen around here."

Chad saw them walk back around the house. He was just as relieved they were leaving. The fire was dying down, and its ebbing might prompt Doolin to investigate further.

He watched the five horsemen until they were out of sight. As yet, Nella hadn't said a word, and surely she had heard what Doolin said.

"Poor Dandy," she said in a faraway voice. "I

raised him from a foal. And they just blew him up." Rage was beginning to firm her voice. "Bill's known me for a lot of years, and yet he didn't hesitate. . . ." She hesitated, seeking the right words.

"You'd become a danger to him, Nella. When it came down to you or him, you didn't have a chance."

"Yes," she said abruptly. "I hope Edith has a lasting headache."

Chad chuckled. Her reaction was normal and healthy. She could think of what she had done without a guilty regret.

"How far was the old Cutter place out of Ingalls?" he asked.

"I don't know," she answered hesitantly. "Five or six miles."

He frowned as he shook his head. "Let's take the best of it and say six miles. Are you ready to do some walking? We've got a lot of it ahead of us."

"To where, Chad?"

"Guthrie. That's the only place I know of where you'll be completely safe." It was funny how a man's attitude could change. Just a while back, he had been filled with bitter resentment of her because of Frank's death. That had ebbed, leaving him filled with more sorrow than hatred. What she had done was understandable. He guessed everybody was caught up in a chain of events they couldn't break.

He made a wide detour of the burning wreckage of the house, not wanting her to see what one of Doolin's men had found: a part of Dandy.

She walked some fifty steps before she said passionately, "I hate him."

"Who?" he asked in mild surprise.

"Bill Doolin. Life doesn't mean anything to him."

Chad considered that, then agreed. "Not when it stands in the way of some purpose of his. It's going to be rough walking. We better not use the road. It's a possibility that Doolin or some of the others might return. We're in danger of being seen by some casual passerby. He could report what he had seen to Doolin."

"Like I did?" she asked bitterly.

He patted her shoulder. "You didn't know any better. You know now." He fell silent. That wasn't what she should be fretting over. She should be worried about all those miles between here and Guthrie. One day's walking wouldn't do it. It would stretch well into the following day. They had no food and only a partial canteen of water. It was going to be one rugged trip.

CHAPTER 9

It was getting onto daylight, for Chad could see the first, false light of dawn. He knew they hadn't made more than three or four miles and, even at that, it would be faster walking than they could do in the daylight. He was afraid most of the daylight hours would be spent in hiding or sneaking furtively along. Nella was having a tough time of it. Keeping off the road made for a lot tougher walking. In the darkness, the small stones and other impediments couldn't be seen. Nella had stumbled several times.

"I guess these shoes weren't made for this kind of walking," she said apologetically.

"You're doing just fine," he said, trying to bolster her spirits.

Nella shook her head. "I'm not, and both of us know it. I'm getting so tired. Chad, why

119

don't you go on ahead? You could make so much faster time. You could come back after me."

In the strengthening light, her face was more distinct. He stared at her in outrage. What did she think he was? He couldn't walk off and leave her to face any possible danger alone. "We'll make it together," he said stiffly.

She smiled faintly. "Did anyone ever tell you you're hard-headed?"

That brought a chuckle from him. "A lot of times. But I never changed."

"Then could we rest a little while, Chad?"

"Sure," he said promptly.

This was possibly the toughest spot she had ever known. No, he thought in quick denial. She was an orphan; she had known distress of the spirit before. Just the same, he wouldn't choose this for any girl.

They sat together, watching the sun come up. "Nella, we won't go on much longer. At this hour there'll be little travel. But during the day we won't be able to travel very much."

"You're still afraid someone will see us?"

"It's still possible," he admitted. "When Doolin gets an idea he holds onto it like a snapping turtle."

That made her shudder. It recalled the bad time of just a few hours past. "I'm ready to go on, Chad," she said.

"Are you sure?" he asked doubtfully. "We could rest a little longer," though he seriously doubted what he said. A brief rest didn't bring back an exhausted person. It took days to achieve that.

"Yes," she said positively.

He helped her to her feet, watching for any indication that she was lying to bolster him. He came a little closer to the road, trying to choose a smoother path. Maybe just a little further and he would insist that she try to sleep.

He cursed that damned sun. At this time of the year, it picked up strength quickly. He could feel the sweat pop out on his face, and he saw the drawn look on Nella's face.

"Let's stop for a while," he said. "I'm not worrying about you," he said quickly. "But I'm giving out."

Her smile eased the drawn look. "I know you're lying, but I'm ready to stop."

He uncapped the canteen before they sat down and held it while she drank. That canteen was heavy for her to handle, though it was getting lighter in weight. He could tell by the increased sloshing of the water. That added another concern to his worries. He would have to find water. So far, he hadn't been able to replenish the canteen.

His face went tight as he heard the sound of horses coming down the road. He wasn't able to spot any yet for the road bent sharply about a hundred yards away, but, from the sound of it, he would see those horses soon.

His eyes darted about, trying to find a hiding place. He had no idea of who those horsemen were, but it could mean imminent danger. His eyes picked out a fairly thick clump of elderberry bushes. An elderberry was a big-leafed plant, and the swooping branches were thickly festooned with large bunches of small white flowers. A little later on, those flowers would turn into small green berries, which by fall would turn into thousands of small black berries. They could be turned into a tasty pie, and an even better wine. Chad knew. He had drunk his share of elderberry wine. Right now he wasn't interested in the wine-making possibility; he was only interested in the concealment those bushes could afford. It could do nicely. Those flower-laden branches bent gracefully almost to the ground, and once a person slithered under them he would be hidden from everything but the most seeking eyes.

He reached down and extended a hand. "Come on! Hurry!" He didn't try to disguise the urgency in his voice.

Alarm filled her eyes. "What is it, Chad?"

"I don't know yet. But don't you hear those horses?"

She listened, then nodded. In her weariness, she hadn't heard them until now.

"Where do we go?"

He pointed at the elderberry bushes. "Once we get under them we'll be safe from all eyes."

If she ached now it didn't show, for she covered the short distance to the bushes with alacrity. He let her wriggle under the low-reaching fronds and followed after her. He squirmed around until he had a better view. The bushes grew so closely together that he had a limited view of the road. He kept his eyes fixed on the small segment of road he could see. The horsemen would pass in that small space.

He saw the near horse first, and he didn't know the man. Then, as the pair passed on down the road, he caught a glimpse of the other horseman. It was a restricted view, but he knew that back well. It was Nix.

He jumped to his feet, clawing his way out of the bushes. He heard Nella's startled cry. "What are you doing?" and paid no attention to it. He had to stop Nix before he got out of earshot.

"Hey, Evett," he bawled. "Evett!"

He had good lungs, and his voice had carrying power. Nix pulled up short and whirled his horse about, his face questioning.

"It's all right," Chad called down to Nella. "I know him. That's Evett Nix, chief marshal of Oklahoma."

He hurried to the edge of the road, waving his arms. Behind him, he could hear Nella's progress, though it wasn't nearly as aggressive as his walk.

"Evett!" he yelled again. "It's me. Chad."

Nix saw Chad, and the startled doubt left his face. He galloped his horse toward Chad, and the other rider followed. Nix pulled up short and said half humorously, half angrily, "Will you tell me what the hell you're doing hiding under a bush?" He saw Nella and said knowingly, "Ah, I see."

The remark put anger on Chad's face. "You don't see a damned thing. Marshal, this is Nella Ellsworth."

Nix bobbed his head in acknowledgement. "This is Curt Lacy," he said, introducing the second rider. "Chad, you're quite a way out of Ingalls."

Chad was suddenly bone-wracking weary. He sighed and said, "And damned lucky to get this far. Nella got me out of a tight bind. If it wasn't for her, I wouldn't be here."

Nix's eyes were kinder as he looked at Nella again. "I'm grateful to you, Miss Ellsworth. But why the hiding?"

"We didn't know who was coming along," Chad explained. "Until I knew, I thought it best to remain hidden."

Nix's eyes sharpened. Something had happened that he didn't know about. He swung down, handed his reins to Lacy, and walked a few paces off with Chad. "You better start at the beginning."

Chad looked back at Nella. He didn't like walking off, leaving her alone. But things would improve and go better after he talked to Nix.

He started with the visit to the drugstore. "Frank was concerned with my cough. He wanted to get something for it. We walked into the drugstore, and Nella was working there. I got acquainted with her."

Nix looked back at Nella. "I can see why."

Chad scowled at him. "You've got a one-track mind."

"I'm not that old," Nix said plaintively, "not to appreciate a good-looking woman."

Chad's scowl grew. "It hasn't been that way at all. The doctor was preparing a corpse for burial. We went into the room where he was working, and it was Ol Yantis."

125

Nix sucked in a breath, and his eyes glinted. "Go on."

"Dr. Swanson knew Bill Doolin. Doolin's been living around Ingalls for some time."

"Ah," Nix breathed. "So my guess was right."

"Yes. Frank and I rented a room from the only hotel in town. Nella knew the owner well. She's her stepsister." He would explain later about the relationship between the two women. "Nella heard Frank and me talking about the Wild Bunch."

Nix looked at her again, and there was a new hardness in his eyes.

"That woman who owns the hotel has some connection with Doolin," Chad went on. "Frank and I went back to the hotel and holed up for the night. Frank guessed we were in trouble. We had a room on the second floor and thought we'd be relatively safe there. They had to come up those stairs to get at us. How wrong we were." His eyes were momentarily bleak. "Those bastards climbed a tree just out-side of the window to our room. They gunned Frank down when we went to the window. I tried to help Frank, and they got me." He gestured vaguely. To quell the concern spreading across Nix's face, he said, "I'm all right. It was only a glancing shot. Frank was still alive when

126

I came to. Before he died, he wanted me to get out of town as fast as I could go. That was the last thing he said." The anguish of his loss had returned, twisting his face. "I couldn't do anything for him. I thought he'd appreciate it if I got the news about Doolin and his gang to you."

"You did right," Nix said explosively. "Then that woman is no more than a common criminal, like all the rest of them."

"Lay off her, Evett," Chad said sharply. "I wouldn't be here if it wasn't for her. When I started to slip out of the hotel, the owner stopped me. She had a gun on me to emphasize what she said. Nella stepped up behind and demanded she drop her gun. She threatened to shoot her if she didn't. Edith must have believed her for she dropped the gun. Then Nella hit her over the head with the barrel." Chad's eyes twinkled as he remembered how ridiculous Nella had looked holding that big gun. "Nella had brought a horse with her. It was a good thing she did — they'd taken the wagon and team. I couldn't have gotten out of Ingalls."

Some of the harshness left Nix's face. "She changed sides in a hurry," he said stiffly.

"Oh, come on," Chad protested. "She didn't know how desperate a man Doolin is. He'd been good to her. Nella didn't say so, but I think the hotel woman might be Doolin's woman. Doolin or one of his gang shot down Dr. Swanson. Doolin didn't like his talkative ways. That changed Nella's mind about him. She loved that old man. He'd given her a job and help when she needed it."

"Did she see the doctor's shooting?"

Chad nodded. "It was done by one of Doolin's gang."

"Would she testify?"

"I think she would. What happened afterwards changed all her ideas about Doolin."

"There's more?" Nix asked incredulously.

"A lot more," Chad replied solemnly. "That horse of hers picked up a stone and went lame. We took shelter in an abandoned farmhouse." A shiver ran through him at the memory of those tense hours spent there. "Doolin and the others knew we went there, or tracked us there."

That incredulous note returned to Nix's voice. "You stood them off? How in the hell did you do that? You weren't armed. Ah," he said, remembering that Nella had held a gun on the hotel owner. "You used Nella's gun?"

Chad shook his head. "I heard a running horse and made a lucky guess. I hustled Nella out of there through a rear window. Kids or someone had broken all the windows out. We barely made it when the place was blown up. That rider tossed in a stick of dynamite. We were sheltered behind some trees. It tore that old house to pieces, then it caught fire."

Nix shook his head. "You had a rough few minutes."

"Rough enough," Chad agreed. "Five of them looked over the burning wreckage. It was too hot for them to get closer. Doolin didn't think it worthwhile to wait longer. He thought the dynamite had gotten us. I'd put the horse in the lean-to against the back of the house. One of that bunch found one of the horse's rear legs. That convinced Doolin there was no use spending any more time looking for us. We started walking back to Guthrie. Nella was plumb worn out. I heard your two horses coming so we hid in an elderberry thicket. I recognized you and yelled." He shrugged. "I was never so relieved to see a familiar person."

"I can imagine," Nix said dryly. "We'll get you back to Guthrie. Now that I know the Wild Bunch is in the Ingalls area, I'll do something about it."

"She's no criminal," Chad said stubbornly.

"Damn it, I can see that now. Let's go back to them."

He walked with Chad to where Nella and Lacy stood. "Nella," he said gravely. "Chad filled me in on everything that's happened. You're a tough and brave little lady."

Tears filled her eyes, and she turned her head so that he couldn't see them. "I learned how wrong one can be about people you think you know. For what Bill Doolin did tonight he deserves to be caught."

"Even if your sister must pay too?" Nix asked quizzically.

Nella tossed her head angrily as though to quell further tears. "We've had disagreements before. She's not really my sister."

"Then it won't hurt you if you're called to testify against Doolin?"

"I'd like the chance," she said with vigor.

Nix grinned. "I didn't lose everything, even if I lost Frank. Let's get back to Guthrie. Would you rather ride behind Chad?"

Nella glanced at Chad and flushed. "I think I would," she said.

"Fine. Chad, you take my horse. I'll ride behind Lacy. We've got to get you two where you can rest." He saw the argument forming in Chad's face and hastened to stop it. "You've done enough. It's time you rest and get your strength back."

"Maybe I should," Chad replied, and sighed.

CHAPTER 10

Guthrie had never looked better to Chad. "I'm going to sleep for a solid twenty-four hours, Evett."

"Excellent idea," Nix approved. "You two come with me to Mrs. Tucker's boarding house. I think she'll find a couple of rooms for you two."

The dark circles under Nella's eyes made them look enormous. She smiled at Chad. "I think I'll beat any record you set for sleep."

Mrs. Tucker was a buxom woman of fading complexion. She listened to Nix's request. "They've done the law a great service, Mrs. Tucker. They need a long rest. Can you accommodate them?"

Mrs. Tucker draped an arm over Nella's shoulders. "You look plumb worn out, you poor little thing. You come with me." She climbed the stairs with Nella, her clucking carrying back to Chad and Nix.

"You won her over in a hurry," Chad remarked. "Mrs. Tucker didn't put up any argument at all." He cocked an eye at Nix. "You must have a way with women."

"Cut it out," Nix growled. "She's a good twenty years older than I am. Besides, I'm already married."

"It don't look to me like you're satisfied. Does your wife know how you feel?"

"Why, damn it," Nix bristled. "Of all the cock-eyed ideas —" He broke off, as he saw that Chad was joshing him. "I'll be glad when Mrs. Tucker gets back and takes you off my hands."

Chad grinned. "What are you planning, Evett?" He howled indignantly as he saw the stubbornness set in on Nix's face. "Damn it, I've got a right to know."

"Not this time." Nix grinned at Chad's increasing rancor. "You need a rest. I heard you say you're going to sleep twenty-four hours."

Chad shook his head. "Not if you're planning something. I'm not that weak. I owe Doolin something for Frank."

Nix could be just as obstinate, and he shook his head. "No way. Now that I know where Doolin is, I can handle it. I lost Frank. I don't figure on losing his brother."

The blood rushed into Chad's face, turning it a fiery red. He had a right to be in the final run-down of Doolin, and Nix was cutting him out.

Mrs. Tucker came back down the stairs, and Nix shook his head at Chad. The gesture warned Chad that he wanted no idle talk spread about Doolin.

"She was worn out," Mrs. Tucker said. "She was asleep before I left the room. Now, I'll show you your room, Mr. Grimes."

Nix followed them up the stairs. Chad wasn't against that. He had a lot more to say to Nix.

It was as nice a room as Chad had ever looked at, and he said so. Mrs. Tucker beamed with pleasure. Chad had to wait until she waddled out of the room before he could resume his argument with Nix. He paced the room as he marshaled his points. "Damn it, Evett. I can shoot. I can handle a Winchester and a Colt. You're treating me like I'm a kid."

Nix sank down into a chair. "I'm not," he exploded. "The way you're pacing, you sure don't look like the man who just said he was going to sleep for twenty-four hours. You've done a good job, Chad. I know about where Doolin is settled in. When I get back, I hope to report to Washington that another famous outlaw is eliminated."

"I do all the spade-work, and you do all the planting and harvesting," Chad said passionately. Nix's stern countenance didn't change, and Chad pleaded. "At least you can tell me what you've got in mind."

Nix stared at him a long moment, then laughed. "I've been in this job too long. I'm doubting everyone. I know I can trust you. I don't think you're likely to hunt up Doolin and tell him what I plan."

He laced his fingers together and stared at the floor. "You and Frank proved that nobody goes into Ingalls without Doolin being suspicious. The second he gets wind of a posse of marshals riding that way, he'll be long gone. I can't give him that chance."

Chad waited impatiently for Nix to continue.

Nix looked up to meet Chad's eyes. "I think I can prevent his running. I'm going to send a messenger to Chief Deputy Hale at Stillwater. I want him to raise at least a dozen men and get ready to ride to Ingalls."

"What's to keep Doolin from getting word you're coming?" Chad burst out.

Nix shook his head ruefully. "Still don't believe I can handle it, do you? I want Hale to put his posse into a covered wagon. There'll be a stranger driving that wagon. I'll be in charge of a similar wagon moving in from Guthrie. Doolin won't know that driver either."

"You planning on driving straight into Ingalls?" Chad asked argumentatively.

"I know Ingalls too," Nix said. "I want to throw up a cordon of men to cut off any avenue of escape. My wagon and party will skirt the town. We'll come in from the south. We'll stop in that thick grove of trees to the north. You've seen it?"

Chad scowled as he laid out the town in his mind. "I know it."

"The men will stay under cover of the canvas of the wagons. We'll be loaded with ammunition, rifles, and six-guns. When we get there, the men will come out and take up positions behind brush, fences, and buildings that line the west side of Ash Street. Hale can come in down Ash Street, stopping just beyond Light's blacksmith shop at the Pierce and Hostetter feed barn." He finished and looked hopefully at Chad.

Chad turned Nix's plan over in his mind. "It could work," he said slowly.

"It will work," Nix said. "This will be the first carefully planned crack at Doolin and his bunch. They'll surrender, or they're dead men. Go on and get some sleep, Chad. God knows you've earned it." At the trace of argument still remaining in Chad's face, Nix burst out, "Can't you see it, Chad? You've done all the preliminary work. In this case, that could be the hardest of all. I know what's in your head. You think I still consider you a kid. You've proven how wrong that thought is; after I take Doolin, I'm appointing you as full marshal on a regular-pay basis. Does that eliminate your doubts?"

"Yes," Chad said grudgingly. "But I'd still like to be in on the final cleanup."

Nix stood and grinned. "Sure you would. But you don't think that getting rid of Doolin will stop all the trouble, do you? After Doolin, there'll be another, then another."

Chad tugged off his boots and lay down. "All those others won't mean half as much to me as Doolin." Lord, his eyes were getting heavy. He'd better lie down before he fell down.

"So long, kid," Nix said, gently closing the door behind him.

Chad had only a few moments to think about what Nix proposed. It was a solid plan; this time, Doolin should either be captured or killed. Killed, Chad thought with an unusual thrust of viciousness. A blanket of sleep blotted out all his thoughts.

Chad was a little disappointed when he

woke. The sun was still out, and by the slant of its rays it wasn't much later than when he went to sleep. Damn, he thought he was more weary than that. But he was refreshed, and he felt fine except for the ravenous reach of his appetite. He slapped his belly and said, "Shut up. I'll see about getting you fed."

He went downstairs to find Nella in the dining room. Her face was a little pale, but her eyes were bright and shining.

"So you couldn't sleep long either," Chad remarked.

She laughed and asked, "What day do you think this is?"

He reflected a moment. It was the day after yesterday. "It's Wednesday," he announced.

"It's Thursday," she said triumphantly. "You slept a whole day away. Don't look so startled. I haven't been up long."

He stared at her. "You're kidding."

She shook her head solemnly. "I couldn't believe it either when Mrs. Tucker told me what day it was. I'm starved. She's fixing something for me to eat. She's in the kitchen now."

"We've missed all those meals," Chad said in astonishment.

She nodded again, her eyes sparkling.

Chad grinned. "Don't be surprised if I wrestle that food away from you. If I missed all these meals, don't expect me to have any manners."

"Did Marshal Nix get away?" she asked, lowering her voice.

"Yes," Chad's grin broadened. "I started to say yesterday. It should be the day before yesterday."

She looked solemn now. "Is he going after Bill?"

Chad nodded. "He's got an excellent plan. This time he won't miss."

"That probably means more bloodshed."

"It does," Chad said firmly. "Nix is a determined man. Unless Doolin decides to give up." He felt a surge of wistfulness. He sure wished he could be in on what would be happening about now in Ingalls.

"I hate that," she said passionately.

"Because of Doolin?" he asked, his face hard.

"No," she denied. "Because of the necessity of shedding all that blood. Bill won't ever give up."

"No," he said soberly. He felt a keen disappointment. She still felt something for Doolin.

She read his expression correctly and shook her head. "I don't care what happens to him. He deserves whatever happens. But all those other men involved don't."

Chad's disappointment disappeared. She had

picked her side. Mrs. Tucker used her hip to bump open the swinging door. Her arms were burdened with a tray stacked with hot, smoking dishes. The smell of those dishes reminded Chad's belly how it had been abused. Mrs. Tucker smiled at Chad. "I thought I heard you come into the dining room. I knew you would be hungry. Do you know how long you've been asleep?"

Chad smiled whimsically. "Nella tells me it's over a whole day. She's wrong, isn't she?"

Mrs. Tucker shook her head. "She's right. This isn't regular mealtime, but Marshal Nix told me to give you two special care. Of course, if you don't want this I can take it all back into the kitchen."

Those dimples reappeared in Nella's cheeks. "That wouldn't be wise, Mrs. Tucker. He just finished telling me he's lost all his manners."

"Good," Mrs. Tucker said. For a moment, she was busy setting the laden dishes on the table. "I'd hate to see all this food wasted."

Chad seized a piece of toast and piled jam on it. "It won't be wasted," he assured her. He stuffed half of the toast into his mouth. For the next several minutes, he was too busy to do any talking.

CHAPTER 11

It was stifling hot under the canvas cover of the wagon. It had been a long, grueling trip, and Nix's butt ached from the constant jolting. The other men crammed into the wagon knew the same discomfort for one of them said bitterly, "Jesus Christ. And we do this for what little money we're paid."

Nix grinned cynically. "Rather be with Doolin, Sam? He gets paid a lot more for a job, but it's not as lasting."

Sam grinned sourly and said, "I guess not."

Nix had a limited view over the driver's shoulder. "Ingalls up ahead. We'll soon be able to climb out."

"I don't think I'll be able to walk," Sam said.

"Then you better learn how to, and fast," Nix counseled. "If you don't move fast, one of Doolin's bullets will find a nest in your hide.

Then you won't be able to walk at all."

Sam pursed his lips. "That's why I like working for you. You're always so encouraging."

Nix chuckled. "I always try to be cheerful." He wished he dared risk another peek, but somebody might just catch a glimpse of someone besides the driver in the wagon. That would blow the whole plan.

He waited a few more moments and asked, "Where are we, Dick?"

"Just passing the Ransom Saloon," the driver answered in a low voice. "Several hard-looking customers standing in the doorway."

"Do they look alarmed, Dick?"

"I'd say more bored."

"Fine. Looks like we drove into Ingalls without disturbing anybody. Keep on going to the grove of trees we talked about."

Dick nodded and clucked to his team. In a few minutes, he stopped in the grove of trees, got down, and said, "Nobody following us." This grove was a favorite camping spot for travelers. "Oh, God damn it," he yelped in anguish.

Nix crawled out of the wagon, spurred on by the intensity in the driver's voice. "What is it?" he asked, his voice tight.

"Would you look at that?" Dick asked in disgust. "Either Bob got his directions mixed up, or he doesn't know where this grove is."

Nix shielded his eyes and stared. He felt like swearing. Dick was absolutely right. Bob hadn't continued on to the grove. He had stopped just past the blacksmith shop at the Pierce and Hostetter feed barn. The outlaws in the doorway of Ransom's Saloon hadn't paid any attention to the first wagon, but they were certainly interested in the second one. One of them left the saloon and sauntered toward the wagon.

"Oh, damn it," Nix cried. "That's Bitter-Creek Newcomb. He's getting his horse. He's going to ride by to see what that wagon is all about."

Several of the marshals crowded around Nix. "Shall we get down there?"

Nix's eyes were intent on the unfolding drama. "Hold it a minute. Deputy Speed just entered the feed barn. He's carrying his Winchester. He's probably covering the occupants in the barn. Oh God, if only there aren't too many of them."

"Usually not more than a couple of men," Dick ventured.

"Then Speed can handle them," Nix said in relief. "It all depends upon what Newcomb does."

Newcomb was halfway to the wagon.

Somebody inside that wagon got nervous and, thinking that their cover was ruined, cut loose a shot at Newcomb. In his haste, the shot was poorly aimed, for Newcomb was unhurt. He whirled his horse and galloped back to the saloon.

"That does it," Nix said grimly. "Let's move."

They broke into a pounding run toward the blacksmith shop. Just as they reached it a boy left the shop, stopped, and stared toward the running men, his eyes big. Then he whipped his head toward the mounted man.

"Corral him," Nix yelled. "Before he puts out a general warning. If they don't already know," he finished mournfully. It had been an excellent plan, and now it was falling to pieces.

Three men ran toward the boy and cornered him before he could escape. Newcomb, looking back, saw what was happening. He turned in the saddle and threw his rifle up to his shoulder. Deputy Speed slammed the butt of his rifle to his shoulder and fired at him. Speed's shot was partially good. It hit the magazine of Newcomb's rifle, tearing it loose. It drove the piece of metal into Newcomb's leg. The pain must have been intense, for he flinched as he pulled the trigger. But he clung to his horse and, bending low, he continued on toward the saloon.

Speed levered another bullet into the chamber. His next shot might have killed Newcomb, but he never got the chance.

Somebody was in the second floor of the hotel. A shot rang out from the north window, hitting Speed in the shoulder. Speed dropped his rifle and tried to make it back to the stable door. He decided the stable was too far, turned, and tried to reach the wagon. The marksman in the upper floor of the hotel fired again. The bullet hit Speed in the back, and he fell. Nix groaned deep in his throat. The unknown marksman forced the marshals into the fight before they reached the positions they wanted. Some of the marshals remaining in the grove fired at Newcomb as he changed his mind and rode past the saloon. He veered his course and drove the horse south out of town. Five men still in the saloon began firing to cover Newcomb's escape. Angry, lethal bees filled the air, preventing the marshals from making an advance. A young man came racing out of the back door of Vaughn's saloon. He hadn't covered three steps when another bullet from the upper floor of the hotel dropped him.

"Damn," Nix muttered.

Dick grunted, "That marksman probably thought he was one of us."

"I'm sorry for him," Nix said bleakly. This fight was only beginning, and already it was costing lives. He put his rifle to his shoulder, aimed at a horse tethered in front of the saloon. He squeezed the trigger, killing the horse instantly. At the surprise touching Dick's face, he said, "One of them might have tried to get away on him."

It hurt to kill a good horse intentionally, but Dick nodded at Nix's reasoning. A bar customer from Vaughn's ran into the street. One of the marshals shot him through the liver, thinking he was one of the outlaws.

"Hold it," Nix roared. "That wasn't one of the outlaws!" This was getting more and more bloody. An innocent man was seriously wounded.

He saw that Newcomb had reached the timber, and the first burst of firing died.

Hale and his men had moved up behind the buildings on the west side of Ash Street, and their firing was now concentrated on Ransom's Saloon.

Nix waved his men to follow him and, crawling slowly, made his way through the brush east of the hotel and south across Second Street behind McMurty's. His men made the perilous passage, and Nix's tension lessened somewhat. They had now reached the livery stable were the outlaws kept their horses.

Nix took a deep breath and roared, "Doolin! You and your men are surrounded. There's no chance of escaping."

The skin tightened over his cheekbones as Doolin yelled back, "Go to hell."

"Cut them to pieces," Nix ordered. Lead riddled the plank building, and Nix couldn't see how the outlaws could survive long under that barrage. That fire was coming from the front and rear. "I'm hit, I'm hit," somebody kept yelling. Nix didn't know who it was.

The outlaws made a bold and daring move. Doolin went first, slipping out a side door that Nix hadn't known about. He was followed by Dalton, Red Buck, then Dynamite Dick and Tulsa Jack. They made a desperate run over the short distance, then whirled after they reached the livery stable. There they started firing again at the deputies.

At the same time, somebody in the front door of the saloon sent bullets toward the beleaguered marshals. He had opened the door only a little way, and his Winchester was against his shoulder. Three deputies fired at him simultaneously. Two shots struck him in the ribs, and one broke his arm. His Winchester dropped across the threshold, and the man fell heavily.

"Who was it?" one of the deputies called.

Nix had gotten a fair glance at the man before he fell. "I think it was Murray. He bartended in that saloon." He cursed fluently. Murray hadn't been on his list.

The daring move by Doolin made Nix change his plans. He waved Heuston to crawl to a position behind a pile of lumber at the back of Perry's store. The new position would let him command the rear door. Heuston was facing south, directly west and in range of the hotel. He was shielded from the view of the gable windows. The marksman inside the hotel knocked the shingles off from the inside, using the barrel of his rifle. The firing position was too high to reach by just standing, but the marksman climbed up on something and sighted along his barrel. He squeezed the trigger and the shot ranged downward through the improvised hole. Heuston fell in a sprawling position. He wasn't dead, for Nix saw him move spasmodically, but he was badly wounded.

Doolin and Dynamite swung up and made a wild dash out of the rear door, heading southwest. Dalton, Red Buck, and Tulsa Jack burst out of the front door, their destination a ravine a few hundred yards away.

As Dalton galloped down the street, Nix

147

fired and hit Dalton's horse in the jaw. It didn't drop the animal, but it spun him around, and he was hard to manage. Dalton had difficulty getting him going again, but he finally managed it. He went perhaps seventy-five yards when Deputy Shadley, trying to score with a long, almost impossible shot, hit the horse in the leg. The horse went down, and Dalton went down on the other side of his horse.

"I got him," Shadley yelled exultantly.

But he was wrong. The fall didn't hurt Dalton and, keeping the wounded horse between himself and the withering fire, he ran onward. He reached a wire fence where the other outlaws were gathered.

Dalton quickly assessed the situation. That fence could get all of them slaughtered. "I've got wire cutters in my saddlebags," he yelled. "I'll get them." He dashed out of a shallow draw, taking the marshals completely by surprise. Dalton weaved and bobbed on the course he took back to his injured horse.

Shadley moved to the south and west of Call's house in order to get a better shot at Dalton. The unseen marksman on the hotel's second floor got back into the fray. The first shot missed Shadley, but it alerted him and he changed his course. A yard fence blocked his way, and Shadley caught his coat on it as he tried to bound over it. That damned fence fought him with the devil's persistence, and he couldn't free his coat. He finally jerked at it in sheer desperation, and he heard the tear of ripping material. It threw him off balance, and he fell. While he tried to struggle back to his feet, the marksman had another shot at him. The bullet slammed into his right hip, shattering the bone. The bone deflected the bullet's course, and it lodged in his right breast.

Shadley managed to reach the Ransom house, begging for assistance. Mrs. Ransom slammed the door in his face, ordering him to get out of here.

"I'm wounded," Shadley said feebly.

"Selph's cave is just a short distance from here," Mrs. Ransom called through the door. "There are several people there, among them Dr. Selph. Maybe he can help you."

Shadley staggered off the porch. He was hit again twice in quick succession. He glanced frantically at Dalton who could barely be seen above the downed horse, as he fumbled at his saddlebags. Shadley lost all thought of shooting Dalton. If he didn't get to the cave in a hurry he knew he was a goner. He weaved a faltering, staggering course toward the cave, almost a block away.

Dalton jerked the wire cutters out of a saddlebag. He paused long enough to shoot his wounded horse in the head, then set out on a dead run toward the obstructing fence. Doolin and the others were still spread out along it, returning fire the marshals sent their way.

Deputy Masterson fired from behind a blackjack tree, where he had worked himself into a favorable position. The tree was a good ten inches in diameter. The trunk was gouged with bullets that had struck above Masterson's head, showing the efficiency of the outlaws' fire. Small twigs and limbs lay on the ground all about him. He swore as he fired his last bullet. He didn't know what held up the outlaws, but if he didn't keep up his fire he was sure they would escape.

He backed away from the tree, turned, and raced to the covered wagon. Bullets hummed around him, but he was untouched. Masterson filled his pockets with cartridges and made his way back to the tree. But, during his absence, Dalton worked on the fence with his cutters. After cutting through, the outlaws rode out of the draw, flogging their horses. Dalton was up behind Tulsa Jack. He turned and steadied his rifle. Nix, Roberts, Steel, and Burke joined in Masterson's fire at the escaping men. One of them got Dynamite Dick, for he tumbled out of his saddle. The other outlaws stopped and lifted Dick back onto the saddle of Doolin's horse. Doolin jumped up behind the wounded man and set the horse into motion again.

"How bad is it?" Tulsa Jack called.

"He got hit in the neck," Doolin answered. "He'll make it."

He headed southeast to the top of a hill and stopped to fire several shots along Oak Street. A teenager too interested in seeing the fight stopped one of those shots in the shoulder. That shot seemed to be the outlaws' last salvo, for they turned their horses and fled.

Nix rushed up to the fallen boy. "I'll get him to the cave," he called. "There's a doctor there."

A great wave of weariness ran over him as he examined the boy's wound. The boy wasn't seriously injured. "What's your name, son?"

"Frank," the boy replied.

"Think you can walk to the cave?"

"Sure," the boy answered. "Wasn't that a hell of a fight?"

Nix's eyes narrowed. It sounded as though the boy had a great admiration for the outlaws. "Do you know who shot you?" he questioned sharply.

"Sure. It was one of the Wild Bunch. I saw

them up on that hill, firing down on the town."

Nix was vexed at the evident admiration in the boy's tone. "You sound like you think what they did was just great."

"Wasn't it?" the boy asked. "You had them outnumbered two to one, and they beat you."

Nix clenched his jaw to keep from snapping at the boy. Here was evidence of the difficult job the marshals faced. The public still backed the outlaws, regardless of their criminal record.

He took the boy to the cave and turned him over to a doctor. The doctor removed the coat and slit the shirt to get at the wound. There was quite a bit of bleeding, but after the doctor's probing he announced, "Just a superficial wound."

"I'm glad for him," Nix said grimly. He walked over to Shadley, who lay in a row of wounded. "How are you doing?"

"Better now," Shadley answered with effort. "When I first got here, the doctor was busy amputating a finger from a farmer who caught it in machinery. That waiting was pure hell, but now I'm resting easier. When the doctor asked about my wounds, I told him that Dalton had hit me three times," he said with a trace of wonderment in his voice. "After his examination, the doctor disagreed. He said those three shots came from a height."

"That damned hotel," Nix burst out. "No wonder he had us pinned down." No wonder everything the marshals tried to do had failed.

Shadley tried to grin and it was a feeble attempt. "Somebody sure cut our combs short," he said wanly. "Did they get away?"

"Every damned one of them," Nix answered moodily. "It almost makes a man believe that God was on their side."

Shadley's eyes brightened. "He wasn't on one of them's side. You remember the one who fell in the saloon's doorway? They just brought him in."

Nix remembered the incident. It had happened at the height of the battle. Whoever it was had given the outlaws a chance to make a successful break for it.

"He's over there with the other wounded," Shadley said. "It's Murray. He was the saloon's bartender."

"I want to talk to him," Nix said grimly.

Murray was a stranger to him, and he asked the doctor which one he was. Doctor Pickering pointed him out. Nix walked up to the prone figure and looked down at him. Murray was in evident pain. He had been hit twice in the ribs, and another bullet had broken his arm.

"Was it worth it?" Nix asked coldly.

Murray looked at him with pain-glazed eyes.

"You didn't take any of them, did you?" he asked through gritted teeth.

Nix shook his head as he turned away. A man like Murray never changed his mind, regardless of how high a price he paid for his loyalty.

Nix stopped for a moment by Shadley. "I'm going to look into that hotel story. Hope you get well in a hurry."

Shadley started to change his position and winced. "Evett, I'd just settle for recovering, no matter how long it takes."

"Good man," Nix said with feeling. A marshal didn't get a hell of a lot of money to go up against men as desperate as Shadley had faced. He'd better get busy and see if there was anything to the report that somebody had fired on the law officers from the hotel.

He collected a dozen men and approached the hotel. A small crowd had gathered before it, and Nix asked, "Anybody see anything unusual happening around this hotel?"

A woman bursting with the importance of her information said excitedly, "I saw puffs of smoke rise from the roof and gable windows."

"From the roof?" Nix asked in amazement.

"Look for yourself," the woman said. "There's a hole in the roof. Somebody could have fired from there."

Nix moved to a more advantageous position where he could get a view of the entire roof. He nodded as he saw the gaping hole. Somebody had knocked off those shingles to get an unimpeded shot at the marshals. He returned to his men and said, "Those shots probably came from the hotel. Scatter out and take it. But move cautiously. If he's still there he's deadly."

They formed a cordon around the hotel and moved slowly, their figures tense against anticipated gunfire. A woman ran out of the hotel, stopping them. "The outlaws were here earlier," she cried. "But they're gone now."

"She's a well-known liar," said the woman who first told Nix about the shooting. "You can't depend on her. Why, she's Bill Doolin's woman. She'd do anything to protect him. I'll go in and see if there's anybody left inside."

"Are you sure you want to?" Nix asked doubtfully. "It could be dangerous."

"I want to," the woman insisted. "I'm tired of living under fear of these kind of men."

She tossed her head at the second woman and walked inside the hotel. She climbed the stairs and found Arkansas Tom Jones in a room at the front. If she was frightened it didn't show.

"You better surrender," she said caustically.

"The hotel's surrounded. All of your friends are gone."

Arkansas Tom grinned whimsically. "I never figured on getting out of this alive." He chortled in delight. "Raised a hell of a ruckus with them, didn't I?"

"You did," she acknowledged. "And now you're going to have to pay for it. Do you know how many marshals are out there?"

"Plenty," he said cockily. "I've knocked a hole in the east roof. It gives me command of the whole town. Before I go I'll take seven of those marshals with me. I've got plenty of shells with me." He patted his jacket pockets, and they clinked.

"Are those your final words?"

Arkansas Tom swore at her. "Can't you understand English?"

"I think you'll be sorry," she said flatly.

His face turned ugly. "You better get out of here before I change my mind and hurt you."

She looked at him a long moment, then backed out of the room. Her face was angry as she heard Arkansas Tom's cackling laughter.

She walked outside, and Nix was waiting for her. "Was he up there?"

"He's up there all right. He did all that firing before. Nothing scares him. He wants to take seven more marshals with him. And he's got

156

the ammunition to do it. His pockets were filled with shells."

"You're a brave lady," Nix said in admiration.

She flushed. "I don't deserve any special credit. I was pretty sure he wouldn't harm me."

Nix shook his head. "You never know what one of those kind will do. I'm glad you're safe. And we know what has to be done."

He raised his voice and ordered the crowd back. "Stay way back," he shouted. "There's going to be plenty of flying lead from now on. I don't want anybody else hurt."

He waited until the watching people withdrew to what he considered a safe distance. "Riddle that hotel," he ordered. "Maybe after he ducks a few bullets he might not think it's smart to be so stubborn."

"It won't do much good, Evett," Masterson said. At the outrage on Nix's face, he said, "We'll be firing at an angle. He can figure that angle and lay low to avoid a hit. Only a ricochet has any chance of getting him."

Nix briefly considered what Masterson said. Masterson was probably right, but Nix had to see what good a few volleys of shots would do. No marshal dared show himself but briefly, for after each volley an answering shot or two came from the second floor of the hotel.

"It's not doing any good," Masterson said after he crawled over to Nix.

Nix didn't want to admit that it didn't look like it was, but he had to agree with Masterson's conclusion.

"Get some dynamite," he said.

"How much do you think it will take?"

Nix considered the question. "Two sticks ought to do the job."

Masterson crawled away to get the dynamite, and Nix watched until he was out of sight. His instructions to Masterson had been to set the sticks under the east side. The rest of them would keep the outlaw busy with covering fire.

Somehow the news got out to Edith about what was going to happen. She was distraught when she rushed up to Nix.

"You can't blow up my hotel," she pleaded. "It's my only way of making a living."

Nix cynically doubted that, but it was hard to turn down a woman, particularly when tears ran down her cheeks.

"If you can talk him out, I'll hold up for a few minutes. You've got to make him understand that unless he surrenders the hotel is coming down around his head."

"I can convince him," she said eagerly. She ran across the intervening distance and disappeared into the hotel.

Nix saw several marshals shake their heads. They had no belief in the woman's ability to talk the outlaw out of anything, but it was worth a try.

Men shifted restlessly as they waited, and the few minutes seemed like an eon. Then Edith appeared in an upper window. "I've talked to Tom," she called. "He's afraid of mob violence, and he doesn't want to be put in chains."

"Neither one will happen to him," Nix called back. Edith disappeared momentarily, then tossed a rifle and six-shooter out of the window. She led the man outside the hotel. He was bleeding in a couple of places.

Nix had never seen a more crestfallen man. "Edith tells me that all the boys are gone," Tom said.

"You mean Doolin and the others?" Nix asked.

Arkansas Tom nodded. "Is it true?"

"They tore out of here a good hour ago," Nix answered. "Got clean away." He had never seen a man wilt so.

"Damn it," Arkansas Tom muttered. "I never thought they'd go off like that and just leave me."

Nix felt no sympathy for the man. "You picked the wrong kind to believe in," he said with brutal candor. He called Sheriff Burdick over, and Burdick took Jones into custody. He asked Marshal Sollers if he could get the prisoner to Stillwater.

Sollers gave that serious consideration. "I can, if the rest don't ambush me on the way."

"We'll see that doesn't happen," Nix said grimly. He pulled a pair of handcuffs from his pocket and started to snap them onto Jones's wrist.

Jones howled his head off. "Edith said I wouldn't be put in chains."

"She was wrong," Nix said in disgust. "Listen to that crowd," he pointed out.

The onlookers were surging forward, and their sympathies had swung. Now that all the fighting was over they no longer felt kindly toward a surviving outlaw.

"Do you want to be turned over to them?" Nix demanded.

"God, no," Jones said, his eyes rolling. "Get me out of here."

Nix and three marshals hustled him into a spring wagon. "Go with it," Nix ordered the marshals. "Keep your rifles ready. They might try something to free him."

"Are you coming?" one of them asked. He couldn't quite keep the note of anxiety out of his voice.

"I'll be following right after you," Nix assured them. "I want to get Heuston and Shadley loaded. Then there's the body of Dick Speed."

He couldn't say he'd come out evenly in this fight. Doolin had lost Jones, and would probably consider Murray as lost. Against those two, one of them a minor figure, Nix had lost three.

He supervised the loading of Heuston and Shadley. Poor Speed didn't take as much care. He wouldn't know what was happening to him. Nix climbed up onto the seat with the driver. The spring wagon was still in sight. Within an hour, Arkansas Tom should be in the Payne County Jail in Stillwater.

CHAPTER 12

Nix would have admitted to anybody that he breathed a sigh of relief when Stillwater came into view. It had been a nerve-wracking trip, everyone half expecting to be jumped by Doolin and the others at any moment. It hadn't happened, and he felt limp with exhaustion. His wagon pulled up behind the spring wagon in front of the jail, and by the time Nix walked into the jail Arkansas Tom was already booked.

One of the marshals had a big grin on his face. "Never saw a man so glad to be locked up. I'm telling you Jones was scared." He pursed his lips. "I was too. I kept seeing Doolin waiting behind every tree, every hummock."

Nix nodded. "I know what you mean. I felt the same way."

By the time he signed the necessary papers and walked back outside, the crowd had grown considerably larger, drawn by the spreading reports of the big fight at Ingalls.

Jack Karnes, a lawyer, walked out with Nix. He was a big, bluff man with a keen sense of justice. Karnes looked out at the people and said, "It seems like we're steadily losing the battle with the outlaws."

Nix's eyebrows rose. "What do you mean?" he asked indignantly. He had known Karnes for quite a few years, but at times Karnes's criticisms got under his skin.

"I mean all you come back with is small fry compared to Doolin and some of the others. You know that's true, Evett."

Nix snorted. He thought of the intensity of that fight, of all the bloodshed, and here Karnes was discounting all that terrible effort. "Maybe we didn't get Doolin this time," Nix said quietly. "But he's hurt. He used to be able to rest in a semblance of peace at Ingalls. That's been stripped from him. I doubt if the people of Ingalls will ever harbor him again. I'm also positive newcomers won't be so anxious to join him. Not after they hear how this fight turned out."

His wrath rose at the skepticism remaining on Karnes's face. "You don't believe me," he cried. "Already, men are leaving for Ingalls. Why do you think they're going there?"

"Bloodshed pulls as many people as it does flies," Karnes said cynically. "They're just going down there to look over the scene of carnage."

"You don't think there's more behind what they're doing?" Nix said hotly. He and Karnes had been engaged in many an argument. Karnes had a sly trick of drawing him out, then moving in quickly when Nix was off balance.

"Not enough to crow about," Karnes replied.

"I'll tell you what some of them are doing. They'll be forming searching parties that will spread through the timber and creek bottoms. The public's outlook is slowly changing. Not too far back, an outlaw was looked on as a daring and brave character. Now people are beginning to look at him for just what he is: a criminal that's costing them money to curb. That's not counting all the innocent blood he's shed."

Karnes shook his head. "I hope you're wrong about one thing, Evett."

"What's that?" Nix snapped.

"That your awakening people don't run across the Wild Bunch. Or there'll be more bloodshed."

Nix couldn't keep his worry from showing. Karnes was so right. Most people weren't trained to handle desperate and deadly men. It took a breed of recklessness to be able to cope with such men. If they hadn't been trained along those lines all the determination and sense of outrage wasn't going to help them any.

Karnes grinned twistedly and whacked Nix on the back. "Hey," he exclaimed. "We're on the same side. I didn't mean to get you so stirred up. Let me buy you a drink to cool you down."

Nix briefly considered the offer, then shook his head. "Too many things to do, Jack. I've got to talk to the undertaker about Dick Speed. Then I've got to get over to the doctor's and see how Heuston and Shadley are coming along."

"You're worried about them, aren't you?" Karnes asked sympathetically.

"Damn worried," Nix replied. "Both Heuston and Shadley had the hell shot out of them in Ingalls."

Karnes shook his head. "I wouldn't have your job, Evett, for all the money in the world."

"I'm just hoping that I live long enough to see the time when marshals aren't needed anymore."

"That day will never come," Karnes stated positively. "There'll always be somebody the government has to go after. You're looking for utopia. Why, that'd mean there would be nothing but saints in this world."

Nix grinned bleakly. "I'm afraid you're right."

He continued on downtown until he reached the undertaker's. The owner met Nix with a sober face. "I have all the arrangements made," he said. "The funeral will be on Sunday. The IOOF and AOUW want the service combined in the Methodist Church. If everybody attends who says he's going it's going to be a lengthy procession."

"It will be," Nix said bleakly.

The undertaker was still in a talkative mood. "From everything I hear, Richard Speed was somebody to be admired."

"He was," Nix said vehemently. "I can't pick out a flaw in the man. He had a good disposition, he was a devoted husband and father, and once he became a friend nothing could change him." Nix was far more loquacious than usual, but this sorrowful occasion had destroyed the dam of his reticence.

"Why do we have to lose men like that?" the undertaker asked mournfully.

"I don't know," Nix replied. He was irritated at himself for his runaway tongue. "I've got a couple of wounded men. I've got to see how they are."

"I pray for their full recovery, Marshal."

"Two of us," Nix grunted. He walked out and headed for the small hospital. This was a grueling period for a man, starting with one death, and then waiting for a possible two more.

A doctor met him in the hospital. "How's Heuston?" Nix asked.

The doctor shook his head. "Not good, I'm afraid. He's losing ground fast."

"Oh, God damn it." The expletive was jerked out of Nix.

The doctor was startled, and he said stiffly, "We've done everything we can."

"I'm not doubting that," Nix said hastily. "But I've already lost a good man. Now I'm faced with the loss of another."

The doctor's face was still sober. "Maybe two," he murmured. "I'm not satisfied with Lafe Shadley. He's not making the progress I'd like to see. He seems to be slipping away from us."

Nix's hands clenched and the fingernails bit into his palms. My God, wouldn't the bill for his abortive attempt to take Doolin ever end? It had started with the loss of Frank Grimes, then in rapid succession Dick Speed and the serious wounding of Shadley and Heuston. Against the dreadful bill, Nix could put the wounding of Murray, the reported wounding of Newcomb, and the capture of Arkansas Tom. He didn't consider it a fair exchange at all. He accepted the sole blame for everything. Hadn't he planned the Ingalls raid? Doolin was still out there somewhere, running free. It'll change one of these days, Doolin, he vowed silently.

Tom Heuston died the same afternoon at four o'clock. Nix was there when the sad event happened. The doctor said, "I never saw a man suffer more excruciating pain. Hours and hours of it. He was a brave man, Marshal."

"He was," Nix said soberly. "Maybe too much so for his own good."

Heuston was buried Sunday. The procession that followed his coffin to the cemetery was the longest ever known in Stillwater. Nix had heard estimates of over fifteen hundred people trudging along after the coffin to pay their homage.

Shadley died that afternoon. Nix stayed around Stillwater until Shadley's remains were taken to a train for Orlando. Shadley was to be shipped home to Independence, Kansas.

He was walking toward the wagon, his shoulders drooping, when Karnes stopped him.

"I don't want any more smart remarks, Jack," he growled.

Karnes gave him a reproachful look. "My

God, what kind of a man do you think I am? After all your grievous losses —"

Karnes meant well, but Nix cut his remark short. "Just keep this in mind, Jack. Doolin has about run his bill to its limit. He's got a lot of settling up to do."

Karnes looked at him with awe-filled eyes. "I'm going to say only one more thing, Evett. I'm just darned glad you're not on my tail."

Nix smiled bleakly. "Just be damned sure you don't break the law, Jack." He wrung Karnes's hand and climbed into his wagon. He was unbelievably weary. And the whole miserable process had to be started all over, unless Doolin and the others fled Oklahoma. They were somewhere out there. The groan came deep from Nix's bowels. The trouble was that he didn't have a single lead that could point him in the right direction. He needed that before he could even begin to look.

CHAPTER 13

Guthrie had never looked so good to Nix. He said his goodbyes to the marshals who had accompanied him, and hurried to his office. He hadn't been gone terribly long, but he supposed things had piled up. He had a stack of mail, most of which didn't bother him, but there were three official-looking letters from Washington. He groaned audibly. He knew what they would be before he even opened them. He read them in his mind's eye. What are you doing about Doolin and the Wild Bunch? Demand that we hear from you immediately.

He laid them on his desk. He would have to get off a long report, and his face was hard as he thought of what he would have to say. There would be no way of disguising the report to placate them. Washington demanded only one standard: success. What had happened at Ingalls wasn't success in anybody's eyes. He would start the report when his mind was clearer. Right now, he wanted to talk to Chad.

He turned up the walk to Mrs. Tucker's boarding house, and she met him as he stepped onto her porch. She opened the door for him, and by the sorrowful look in her eyes, Nix knew she had heard of his failure at Ingalls.

"I'm sorry for you and the others," she breathed.

"So you heard about it?" he grunted.

She shrugged those plump shoulders. "You know how things spread. The news is all over town."

"So Chad has heard about it, too?"

"I imagine he has," she answered.

"What did he say about it?" he persisted.

"He didn't bring it up, and I thought it was wiser not to mention it."

Nix nodded dully. Maybe that was best, but it was no permanent solution. It would have to be talked about. "Is he in?"

"Not at the moment." she replied. "He and Nella went out somewhere about the town. By now, I think they know every nook and cranny of Guthrie. They're really enjoying themselves." Her eyes twinkled. "You know, I think something is happening between those two."

Nix could guess at what that was, but he didn't comment. Those two were about the same age. Thrown together the way they had been it wasn't surprising that they should fall in love. Nix sometimes wondered why this life was set up the way it was. Men fell in love while others died. Speed had known that same wonderful feeling, then everything was snatched from him. It had been the same with Heuston and Shadley. Nix couldn't put his finger on what was wrong, but there was a whole lot of unfairness in the scheme.

"They might not be back for hours," he said. Lord, his legs were achingly tired. He was loathe to move.

"They've been gone for hours," she said. "You look so weary. Are you hungry?"

Nix shook his head. He should be; he hadn't eaten regularly, and the food wasn't good. But he was strangely indifferent about eating a meal. "I'm not hungry," he said. "I'll be back a little later on. I want to talk to Chad."

He started to rise, and she placed a hand on his forearm. It seemed like a great weight, holding him in place.

"You could drink a cup of coffee," she persisted.

"That sounds good," he replied. It was an

excellent excuse for him to sit here a little longer.

She bustled out into the kitchen, and it wasn't long before he smelled the aroma of boiling coffee. It smelled good. He sat there trying to make his mind a blank, though thoughts kept slipping in, most of them centered on how he would relate this failure to Washington. His face hardened. Yes, and to Chad. Would there be accusation in Chad's eyes? Nix squirmed inwardly. There possibly could be.

Mrs. Tucker came into the dining room again, carrying a tray, a coffee pot on it, two coffee cups, with sugar and cream.

"Say," Nix exclaimed. "That smells good. Just black, ma'am."

Mrs. Tucker's head turned to one side at the sound of voices at the front door. "Somebody just came in," she said. "I'll bet it's Chad and Nella. I'll tell them you're here." She hurried out of the room.

Nix filled his coffee cup and slowly sipped at it. It was excellent coffee. He just wasn't in any position to give it his full approval. He grew tense as he heard people talking and laughing at the front door. Would that laughter fade from Chad's eyes when he saw them? It could. Nix better get used to accusation from a lot of sources.

Mrs. Tucker let the couple precede her into the dining room. Nix caught the rosy blush in Nella's cheeks, the sparkle in her eyes. It took no prophet to predict that these people were in love. If not yet, then very close to the verge.

Chad's face lighted as he saw Nix, and he strode forward. "Evett," he said. "Mrs. Tucker didn't tell us you were waiting here." He grabbed Nix's hand, and there was no holding back in his grip.

"Good to see you again, Chad," Nix said quietly. He turned his head toward Nella. "Yes, and you, Nella."

Her face had gone taut, and the sparkle had disappeared from her eyes. She seemed like a wary animal, waiting for the unexpected to happen, and half knowing it would be for the worse. A moment ago, they had enjoyed the heights of a dream world, and now it seemed to be gone. Nix mourned the fact that the realities of life always reappeared to eliminate the happier things.

"Coffee's hot, Chad."

Chad sat down, Nella beside him. His eyes had changed, too. They were intense, as though waiting for Nix to say he'd hang himself.

"I need some more cups," Mrs. Tucker said. "I'll be right back."

Chad didn't even turn his head at her departure. "I heard about it, Evett. A lot of guesses mixed up with the talk. You know how those guesses can blow up things."

Nix grimaced. Yes, he knew. Give tongues a few facts and before those tongues were finished they had built up a mountain where before a small hummock had existed.

"Not too many guesses in this," he said quietly. "I fell flat on my face." His face reddened, but he kept resolutely on. "I had one of the biggest failures of my life."

"Want to talk about it, Evett?"

Nix could no longer detect any friendliness in Chad's eyes at all. He raised his hands and let them fall helplessly. "I failed, Chad. As simple as that. I take full responsibility for the whole mess."

Chad's face was tighter as he leaned forward. "You thought of the plan. You weren't the only man in on it."

Was that forgiveness in his voice? Nix didn't know. "No," he said, shaking his head. "It was all mine from the beginning. I had to find Doolin. At a rumor of him being seen around Ingalls –" He broke off, wincing. He hadn't wanted to bring up the first unfortunate part of his plan. Chad would remember that too well.

Nix refilled his cup and sat there, marshaling

his thoughts. All he wanted to do was to tell it exactly the way it had happened.

He took a long swallow and went on. "It was a solid plan, Chad. Once I located Doolin and the Wild Bunch I planned on taking enough marshals to surround him and make him surrender. The last report I had of him was that the bunch were in that hotel. Once we surrounded it with superior numbers, Doolin wouldn't be foolish enough to fight against such odds." Retelling it brought back the heavy, distressed look to his face. "Things went wrong from the start. Two wagons, loaded with marshals, were to meet in that grove of trees. One wagon made it. The other driver got lost or didn't know where the grove was. He drove into town, and it aroused some suspicions. Newcomb came down the street to investigate what that wagon was doing there." His face contorted with a rush of passion as he relived the unfortunate events. "One of my own men got an itchy finger and let loose a shot at Newcomb. That touched off the whole damned fight." He sank into a moody silence.

"Still don't see why you blame yourself," Chad said thoughtfully.

"The man in charge takes blame for all slip-ups. If his planning is sound he'll be prepared for anything."

Chad grinned twistedly. "You're a hard man on yourself, Evett."

Nix shook his head. He took a deep sigh and went on. "Even then, I thought we had them corraled in Ransom's saloon. By God, both sides threw enough lead to fight a war."

"You mean Doolin and the others fought their way out of the trap?" Chad asked incredulously.

"They did," Nix confirmed bitterly. "That bartender did a brave thing. He risked his life, giving Doolin a chance to escape. He opened the front door a crack, firing through it and forcing my men to take cover. Doolin and the others escaped through a side door I didn't know anything about. Another flaw of judgment," he said harshly. "I should have known everything about that town."

"How could you have?" Chad protested. "You didn't live there. How many times had you seen the town: two or three times?"

Nix slashed the air with the edge of his palm. "I should have known. Men's lives depended upon my knowing."

Chad shook his head, but he didn't speak. He waited a moment, then said. "Do you want to talk anymore about it?"

"Yes," Nix said harshly. Once he had started he wanted to get it all out, then maybe he could know a little peace. "One of the outlaws stayed in the hotel on the second floor. I didn't know about that either. Somebody was cutting us to pieces, and I kept thinking it was one of the outlaws on the ground. Dalton's horse was shot from under him. The others fought their way to the livery stable." He stopped, his eyes blank as he recalled that harrowing scene. "I should have known," he muttered.

Chad didn't push him further. Nella's face was white and strained. She had listened, fascinated, to Nix's account of the fight. A little whimpering sound escaped her.

"Stop it," Chad commanded. "You didn't know how desperate those men were."

"But I started all this," she protested in a barely audible voice.

"Oh, dear God," Chad said in disgust. "You and Evett should get together. Maybe you could thrash out who's the most to blame."

"Don't jump on her," Nix said wearily. "She didn't realize what she was dealing with. She more than made up for that mistake." It was amazing, the change in Chad. Before that fateful trip started, he hadn't been anything but a kid; sometimes happy-go-lucky, sometimes petulant. Now his face was composed. He had gained something, and Nix searched for the answer until he came up with it.

Maturity. That was it.

"Before we finally figured out where the shots that did us so much damage were coming from, I had one man dead and two more wounded. Those two died in Stillwater. I saw them buried."

"Go on, flog yourself," Chad said. "You finally got that outlaw out, didn't you? You did, or you wouldn't be here now."

"We did," said Nix crisply. "But not before Doolin and the bunch got their horses and escaped." A wondering note crept into his voice. "They were brave men at that. They risked everything."

"No. They weren't brave. They were cornered rats. A cornered rat fights to the last to escape."

"How did you get that outlaw out of the hotel?" Nella asked in a faint voice.

"A woman was brave enough to go up there and confirm the fact that he was up there, shooting down at us. How she knew or guessed he wouldn't shoot her down amazed me," Nix went on. "We riddled that hotel. And he still refused to surrender. We were shooting upward, and the angle was favorable to him. When he finally quit, he was bleeding from a couple of superficial wounds. I guess a ricochet got him a couple of times."

"Then how come he decided to quit?" Chad asked.

"Edith," Nix glanced at Nella. "Your stepsister finally went up there to try and talk him into quitting. I was ready to blow up her hotel with a couple of sticks of dynamite."

That touched a responsive chord in Nella. "I was wondering how she reacted to all this," she murmured.

"She begged me not to destroy her hotel. It was the only way she had of making a living. She went up and told Arkansas Tom Jones that the others were gone. That crumpled him more than anything else. He threw down his rifle and pistol, came down, and surrendered. I handcuffed him and had him driven to Stillwater. He's there in jail now. He'll face at least three charges of murder."

He was silent so long that Chad hated to push him into further talk. "Will a judge consider what he did as murder?"

"I'd bet on it," Nix said harshly. "I know what you're going to say. But he wasn't fighting for his life when he first wounded Shadley. No, he'll pay for it." He fell silent again, staring at the far wall. God, the mind had too much of a retentive power to recall every little detail. He looked up at Chad and said firmly, "That's about all. I lost three good men. A couple of civilians were killed. How many more were wounded I don't know. A town was thoroughly shot up. Do you still think I shouldn't call it a failure?"

Chad grinned for the first time.

"What do you find so funny?" Nix asked crossly.

"You," Chad replied, and his grin grew broader. "Doolin had a big standing around Ingalls, didn't he?"

Nix nodded. "People almost worshipped him. He spent big chunks of his loot in Ingalls. He was a big help to Ingalls's economy."

"Now he's on the run."

Nix briefly closed his eyes. "I wish to God I knew where. It'll probably take weeks to get another lead on him. I'll have to have it before I can begin to finish this mess. And I've got to report it all to Washington."

"Will you take some advice from a green kid?"

Nix nodded, his eyes narrowed. Nothing Chad could say would bother him. He had said it all to himself.

"You got no reason to hang your head. I say you did a hell of a lot of good. You ran a bunch of notorious outlaws from their holes. They'll have to find some place to reestablish themselves, and they're bound not to feel nearly as secure."

Some of the gloom left Nix's soul. What Chad was saying could be right. He would like to be able to think so.

"I want to walk back to the office with you," Chad said. "We've got some private business to attend to."

Nix knew what Chad wanted. He had promised to give Chad a full commission as marshal. But that was before the Ingalls raid. He shook his head. "We can settle it all here, Chad. I'm not appointing you as a marshal."

Chad looked shocked. "I hate to say this, but you're either a liar or a breaker of promises. Don't you remember what you told me and Frank right before we started for Ingalls? It looks like you're going to have to make a choice: lie or break a promise."

Nix's face burned. If they were alone it would be bad enough to have to take this kind of talk from Chad. To have the two women listening made it doubly worse. "Wait a minute," he roared. "Can't you see that I'm thinking of you? What I did got Frank killed. I don't want the same thing happening to you."

Chad's eyes were hot. "My brother being killed is the reason I want this job so bad. Or do you still think I'm just a kid?"

Nix used scorn in trying to deter Chad. "Suppose I do pin a badge on you? Do you think a lone man can get anywhere against that bunch? I told you how many I had against Doolin in Ingalls."

All the logic in the world wasn't going to erase that hard, determined look from Chad's face. "I want that job," he insisted stubbornly.

Nix could stand firm, or be known as a man who broke his word. Oh, it would get out. The two women would probably see to that. He looked at both of them. Nella's eyes were pleading with a sort of sickness, and Nix instinctively knew that she didn't want Chad to have the job. Mrs. Tucker looked sort of blank, as though everything was happening too fast for her.

Nix sucked in a deep breath. He had never broken his word in his life, and he resented Chad pushing him into a hole like this. He saw a ray of light, and his expression lightened. Even if he commissioned Chad, what good could he do? He would be a lone man; even with the authority of the badge he was practically helpless. He wouldn't have the slightest idea of where to locate Doolin, and Nix could see that Chad's assignments were practically useless. He could keep him out of trouble.

His face turned raw and violent. "No man ever accused me of breaking my word," he said savagely. "If that damned badge is that important to you, you'll get it. Come on. We're going down to the office." He got to his feet and strode out of the room.

Chad hesitated long enough to say to Nella, "I'm going to be just fine. I've got no intentions of getting myself killed."

Two slow tears leaked out of her eyes. "You'll be trying to find Bill Doolin, won't you?"

He grinned lazily at her. "That sorta fits in with my plans," Chad said. "I owe Frank something."

She shook her head in a desperate gesture, and now the tears flowed faster. "You heard Nix say what happened in Ingalls? The same thing could happen to you. You don't realize what you're going up against."

The grin remained on Chad's face, but the eyes were cold and remote. "I think I know." His voice was clipped. "But it's something I have to do."

At her little wail of distress, he went around the table and brushed her forehead with a kiss. "Quit it, Nella," he admonished. "I can take care of myself. We got out of Ingalls, didn't we? Things looked pretty rough, didn't they?"

Mrs. Tucker was watching it all, and Chad didn't care. He pulled Nella to her feet and wrapped his arms about her. "Stop it," he commanded her. He tilted back her face and kissed her. "I'm going to be just fine. Can't you see that I have every reason to get back here? You'll be waiting."

His kiss didn't stop her sobbing, and he held her tighter, trying by physical pressure to stop her crying. "Seems like you should know me well enough to trust me by now," he grumbled with mock indignation. He pushed her back into the chair. "You just wait here. I'll be back. Trust me."

That stunned look remained on Mrs. Tucker's face. "Everything is going to be all right, Mrs. Tucker. Watch out for her, will you?" He winked at Mrs. Tucker, turned, and walked toward the front door. All the way there, he could hear the muffled sounds of Nella's crying. Now he would find out how good he was at keeping promises.

CHAPTER 14

Nix was watching for Chad on the walk outside the boarding house. He was still angry for he raked Chad with burning eyes.

"Sorry I kept you waiting," Chad apologized. "I had to say something to Nella."

Nix went straight to the crux of what bothered him. "Does she approve of what you're doing?" he snapped.

"No," Chad admitted. "But it's just something I have to do."

Nix snorted and started out with long, angry strides toward his office. Chad had no trouble keeping up with him. He was longer-legged than Nix.

Nix was silent until they'd almost reached the office.

"Why don't you say what's eating you and get some relief?" Chad asked, and grinned.

"You're a damned smart alec," Nix fumed. "You got me in a hole, and stomp on my fingers every time I try to climb out."

Chad's grin didn't fade. "I just reminded you of what you promised."

"Yes, and before witnesses," Nix raved. "What good is this commission going to do you?"

Chad sighed. "You still trying to weasel out of your promise?"

"Oh, God damn it . . ." Nix started. He cut off the rest of his words, and his jaw jutted forward. He unlocked the office door, stalked into it, and flopped down into his familiar chair. Chad sat across the desk from him. Maybe it was possible to still reason with him, but Nix would have to keep his words mild.

"Chad, when I made that promise I planned on Frank coming back. His going changed everything."

"Not to me," Chad said stubbornly.

Nix glared at him. "Hardest-headed kid I've ever known. What do you think you can do alone? When all those marshals I had with me couldn't do anything?"

"You pointed that out to me before," Chad said stiffly.

Nix could feel an explosion rising up within

him, and he throttled it down with a harsh hand. "I know how you feel, Chad," he said in a milder tone. "I feel as bad as you do about losing Frank. But what can you do about it now? You can't be a self-appointed destroying angel to go after Doolin. He and his bunch have scattered. It could be a long time before he surfaces again." He wanted to swear. He wasn't reaching Chad at all. There wasn't a crack in that hard mask.

"If I do get a crack at him, my badge would make it official. I just want to be ready. Of course, if you're thinking of breaking your promise . . ." Chad's shoulders rose and fell, and the words died.

Nix could feel the heat rising in his face again. Damned stubborn, hard-headed kid. "Stand up," he snapped. He got a Bible and said, "Place your right hand on the book and repeat after me." He read the vow to Chad, and Chad intoned the words with no inflection in his voice.

"You are now a United States deputy marshal," Nix said in a frozen voice. "That doesn't mean you can do as you see fit. You're still under my command."

A glimmer of a smile touched Chad's face. "Never had any other thought in mind, Evett."

Nix looked suspiciously at him. Damn, but

he wished he could read Chad's thoughts. "I mean it," he said in a stern voice. "Don't leave Guthrie for any reason. I'll pick where you go."

"Why sure, boss," Chad drawled. He tapped the shining badge Nix had pinned to his shirt. "I won't disgrace this, Evett."

"I hope not," Nix said coldly. Chad's evident pride in the new badge shone in his eyes. Chad had two drives that worried Nix: the burning desire to avenge the death of the brother he loved, and a young man's belief that nothing bad could happen to him. He believed he could go after Doolin without adverse results. Nix had seen Chad handle a gun. Chad was good, but he was no expert compared to Bill Doolin. "I want you reporting in here every morning," he said in a stern voice. "Chad, I mean that."

Chad grinned slowly. "I'll be waiting for you at the door every morning, Evett."

"See that you are," Nix grumbled.

Chad walked to the door and flipped a careless wave at Nix. Nix's eyes were moody a long time after Chad left the office. Did Chad mean what he had just said, or was there a devious plan in his head? Nix wished he knew.

CHAPTER 15

Nella's appearance worried Mrs. Tucker. Her face was so distraught, her eyes on the wild side. "Don't worry, honey," she said soothingly. "Nothing's going to happen to him."

Nella blinked furiously to keep the tears back. "You don't know him like I do," she sobbed. "When he gets a purpose in his head nothing will turn him."

"What purpose is that, dear?"

"Getting his badge, then going after Bill Doolin. You don't know how deadly Bill Doolin is. He won't give Chad the slightest chance. He'll cut Chad down —" She snapped her fingers. "Just like that."

Mrs. Tucker looked startled. "Maybe you're guessing wrong."

"I'm not," Nella said between sobs. "He'll

keep searching until he finds Doolin."

"That's not likely. According to Marshal Nix, the outlaws have scattered. How does Chad know where Doolin is?"

"He'll keep looking until he finds out where Doolin is." Nella chewed on her lower lip. "I've got to do something to help him."

"You?" Mrs. Tucker scoffed. "What could a little bitty gal like you do? You better hadn't let Chad hear you say something like that."

Nella's lips were a thin line over a resolute chin. "I might be able to help him," she exclaimed suddenly. She slumped as though there were no longer any moral fiber left in her. "No, I can't," she despaired. "I'd need a horse, and a pair of field glasses. Yes, and a rifle."

Mrs. Tucker eyed her suspiciously. Maybe that wildness in her eyes was an indication that she had let go inwardly. "What do you want with them things?" she asked bluntly.

Nella shook her head. "I've got to do something."

Mrs. Tucker watched Nella tear herself to pieces until she could no longer stand it. "Honey, you've got to stop this. You've got . . ."

Nella stared at her with blank eyes. If she heard Mrs. Tucker none of the words were registering.

Mrs. Tucker could no longer stand to see Nella suffer like this, and she gave in. Maybe it was wrong to help this girl out by doing something she didn't even know about, but Mrs. Tucker's big, warm heart would do anything to let this girl know a little peace.

"Honey, maybe I can help. When Mr. Tucker died three years ago, I thought I'd go to pieces. When a woman loves a man, she'll do anything she can to make things easier for him. That opportunity was snatched from me by Mr. Tucker's death. I scraped up enough money to buy this boarding house, thinking the busier I kept myself the better off I'd be." A tinge of exasperation crept into her voice. Nella still stared at her as though she didn't understand a word. "Nella, do you hear what I'm saying?" she cried.

"I hear," Nella said dully. "I'm sorry, but I don't see where any of this is helping me."

"That's what I'm getting to," Mrs. Tucker said, a bite in her tone. "Mr. Tucker was an avid hunter. Every fall, he went out and tried to get himself a deer." Her face softened. "He wasn't very successful, but he tried. He cherished that horse of his, and his rifle was a prized possession. He had a pair of glasses. I kept all those things in memory of him."

Nella was visibly brightening. "You mean

you've got all those things?" she gasped.

Mrs. Tucker nodded. "I keep Alexander out in the shed in the back of the house. A thousand times I've accused myself of being a fool. All that horse does is eat his head off. But I couldn't bear to think about giving him up. It'd be like breaking an actual tie with Mr. Tucker. He loved that horse so." She started to say something else, then stopped. That girl must be losing her mind; she was laughing and crying at the same time.

Nella managed to get control of herself. "Mrs. Tucker, I'm not laughing at you. Here I thought it was impossible to get the things I need so badly, then you say you have them."

Mrs. Tucker nodded. "Just like I told you."

"Could I borrow them from you? I promise to bring them all back unharmed."

Mrs. Tucker's eyes narrowed. "You've got something in your head, girl?"

"Yes," Nella admitted. "You've given me a way to save Chad. But I can't tell you."

That miffed Mrs. Tucker. "I think you could trust me," she observed.

"It's not that I don't trust you," Nella said slowly. "But in some way you might tell Chad where I've gone. And that could ruin everything." Her eyes slowly filled with tears. "Don't you know how it is to care for a man so much you'll do everything to help him?"

That was a shrewd blow, for Mrs. Tucker caved in completely. "You wait here. I'll be right back with the field glasses and rifle."

She came back a few moments later, holding the objects. Her fingers had a caressing touch as she handed each one over to Nella. "Those are good glasses," she said. "Mr. Tucker didn't have a lot of money to spend, but he threw all caution aside when it came to his hunting."

"They look expensive," Nella murmured. She extended the other hand to take the rifle. Her eyes gleamed. She knew a good gun when she saw one. "I'll probably never fire this," she said. "But I might need it for self-protection."

"Can you handle a gun?" Mrs. Tucker asked in astonishment.

"Yes," Nella admitted modestly. "I'm no stranger to them."

The more Mrs. Tucker knew Nella the more surprise she found in this sprig of a girl. "Do you want to see Alexander?"

"I sure do," Nella breathed.

Mrs. Tucker led her out to the shed. She had had someone build a manger in the small structure.

"Oh, he's a beauty," Nella said, her eyes shining. The horse was a glossy bay, perhaps too fat. This little excursion would probably do him a lot of good.

"Lord, the money I spend on him," Mrs. Tucker sighed. "Sometimes I ask myself why I don't get a little sense and sell him."

"Because you love a man," Nella said, and smiled.

Mrs. Tucker impulsively threw her arms about her. "You do know, don't you? That's why you're doing this. There's Mr. Tucker's saddle and bridle over there." She jerked her head toward the saddle on a rack built by the same carpenter who had constructed the manger. A saddle blanket was folded over it, and the bridle hung from a nail above. Both showed evidence of care. The leather was shiny and soft.

"You spend a lot of time out here, don't you?" Nella guessed.

A faint blush burned in Mrs. Tucker's cheeks. "Don't laugh at me," she said, threatening. "But when I got so lonely I couldn't stand it I came out here and worked on them. Somehow, it reestablishes my connections with Mr. Tucker."

"I wouldn't laugh," Nella said earnestly. "I promise I'll take the best care possible of everything."

"You can ride?" Mrs. Tucker asked, her amazement growing.

"I used to ride a lot," Nella replied. "I owned a fine horse once. He died."

Mrs. Tucker's eyes caught the swelling lump in Nella's throat. The death of that horse must have been painful. "You can't ride in that dress," she said sharply. "Come back in the house. I think Mr. Tucker had a pair of pants that would come close to fitting you. Lord, anything I have would be far too big for you."

She led Nella back into the house and went into a back bedroom. She rummaged in a drawer and pulled out a pair of pants. They were close to Nella's size, but even at that Mrs. Tucker had to poke another hole into the belt, allowing Nella to draw the pants up more tightly.

Nella surveyed herself and giggled like a small child. "I'm glad Chad isn't seeing me looking like this." Her face sobered, and there was that tight, drawn look again.

"What is it, dear?"

"I was just thinking I'll need two more things to make my trip possible."

"Name them," Mrs. Tucker said promptly.

"I'll need a canteen. . . ." She hesitated.

"Mr. Tucker had an old canteen he carried with him on his hunting trips. It's sound. What's the other?"

"I'll need some money," Nella confessed.

"Not a lot. Just enough to buy food to last me on the trip."

Mrs. Tucker's face didn't change. "How much do you need?"

It took effort to get the sum out of Nella's mouth. "Ten dollars," she said faintly. "Is that too much?"

Mrs. Tucker laughed. "I was expecting to hear a much bigger amount."

Nella shook her head, and she looked relieved. "No. Ten dollars will be enough."

Mrs. Tucker handed her a ten-dollar bill, and Nella said, "I can't tell you how grateful I am for this." She folded the bill and thrust it into her pants pocket. "I guess I should be leaving."

"Chad said he'd be back shortly —" Mrs. Tucker stopped abruptly. Nella was vigorously shaking her head.

"The last thing I want is for him to see me before I leave. I'll see him when I return."

Mrs. Tucker walked out with her to the shed. Nella caressed Alexander a moment before she smoothed out the saddle blanket. Mrs. Tucker's eyes widened when Nella muscled that big saddle onto the horse's back. Whoever would have thought that this slip could handle a saddle like that? The horse was docile and made no objection to Nella saddling him. She had her most trouble getting the saddle cinched. "He must have put on weight," she said. "Or he's holding his breath." She drove a small fist into Alexander's belly, and he made a loud whoosh. Nella tried pulling up the cinch strap again. "He wasn't holding his breath." She grinned. She adjusted the bridle over his ears, and Alexander obediently opened his mouth.

"I think he likes you," Mrs. Tucker observed.

Nella stroked the velvety muzzle. "Oh, we'll get along just fine." Her mind was busy with her planning. Bill Doolin hadn't been seen since the Ingalls fight. He must be hiding until the uproar settled down. Nella had picked out a place in her mind. It had to be the old Ellsworth farm where she had been raised. Edith would be there, and Doolin would be drawn to his wife. It was entirely possible that Bill would pick out the farm to lay low. It was about forty miles northeast of Ingalls, and Nella remembered it well. It had never been very profitable, and its appearance showed it. It was an ideal spot for a noted outlaw to hide until he was sure all marshals were out of the area. Nella frowned as she considered another imponderable. Had some of the bunch picked the same place to hide? No, she decided. That would put Edith's parents in jeopardy, and Bill wouldn't want to do that. The farm deserved watching. It would be a long and arduous trip, but she should be able to make it in the time she specified. All she wanted to do was to verify with her own eyes where Doolin was hiding. She didn't think she would be running any undue risk. She could lay a safe distance away from the farm and observe everything that went on through the field glasses. Once she got sight of Doolin, she could slip away and get back to Alexander as quickly as possible. She grimaced at one thought: she wouldn't fare too well during those days. A diet of jerky palled in a hurry, but it would keep the pangs of hunger away, and it was easy to travel with. She would have to stop at a grocery store before she left Guthrie and purchase a supply.

She raised her hand in a farewell wave. "God bless you," she said softly.

Mrs. Tucker couldn't keep the anxiety off her face. "You be careful," she warned. She thought of telling Chad this, and her lips trembled. "What am I going to tell Chad?"

Nella laughed easily. "Tell him I'm gone. What can he do if he doesn't know where?"

Mrs. Tucker visualized Chad's wrath. "He can raise hell," she said grimly.

Nella laughed. "We've handled that before, haven't we?"

She walked Alexander out of the shed, looked once more at Mrs. Tucker, and raised her hand again. "Come on, fatty," she said to the horse. "We're going to take some of that off." She drummed her heels against his flanks, and Alexander responded willingly enough. She had one more stop to make at the nearest grocery store before she set out for the Ellsworth farm.

Chad was pleased with himself. Every now and then he grinned at the shining new badge pinned to his shirt. He was whistling when he opened the door of the boarding house. The anxiety on Mrs. Tucker's face swept the gaiety away. "Where's Nella?" he demanded sharply. Instinctively, he knew that whatever was bothering Mrs. Tucker involved Nella.

Mrs. Tucker licked her lips. "She's gone, Chad," she said faintly.

"I can see that," he retorted crisply. "But where? And when will she be back?"

Mrs. Tucker wrung her hands. She felt so helpless at the crisis that rushed at her.

"I don't know," she said. She wanted to wail, and her hands were shaking. "She wouldn't say."

"She went shopping," Chad said, his relief showing. In their excursions about town, Nella had talked often about what she wanted to buy for him. That was it. Nella had seen something she wanted to purchase. His frown wiped out the relief. To the best of his knowledge, Nella had no money on her. "I'm going out to look for her," he declared.

To his amazement, Mrs. Tucker was shaking her head. "I don't think you'll find her in Guthrie."

Chad scowled at her. "What do you mean?"

"I loaned her Mr. Tucker's horse. She said this was something she had to do, that it would be considerable help to you."

A thought made Chad's stomach feel hollow. The biggest thing she could do to help him was to locate Bill Doolin. But surely Nella wouldn't do anything that rash. Even if she had an idea of where she might locate Doolin, she wouldn't try to capture him alone.

"Didn't she say where she was going?" he demanded.

She shook her head. Those fierce eyes were boring into her, making her feel faint. "She said if I didn't know I couldn't tell anyone."

"Oh, God damn it," Chad burst out. He turned to plunge out of the house. Her question stopped him at the door. "Where are you going?"

"To see if I can't find out where she went," he flung back over his shoulder. "I want to tell Nix about this."

Mrs. Tucker sat down weakly in a chair. She wanted to cry. The only thing she had been right about in this whole mess was her saying that Chad would be wild when he learned Nella was gone. She shivered at the memory of his eyes. He was wild, all right.

Chad burst into Nix's office, his entrance jerking Nix's head up from some paperwork.

"I'll say one thing, Chad. You make your trips short. You look wild. What bit you?"

"Nella's gone," Chad burst out.

Nix's jaw dropped. "What do you mean, gone? If she wasn't at the house, she's only out for a few minutes."

"More than that," Chad said hoarsely. "When I said gone, I meant gone. Mrs. Tucker told me about it."

Nix swallowed hard. "You mean for good gone?"

"That's the gone I mean," Chad said furiously.

"Jesus," Nix said in a small voice. "When I saw you two together, I had the impression everything was going just fine."

"I thought so too," Chad said bitterly. "Mrs. Tucker had a horse left by her husband. Nella borrowed it. She told Mrs. Tucker to tell me she'd be back in about a week."

"You see?" Nix said triumphantly. "You come storming in here, raising hell over nothing. She went to visit some friend or a relative."

"No," Chad said violently. "It's far worse than that. She knew how badly I wanted to run Doolin down. She got some crazy idea in her head that she might know where he is. She's gone to see if her idea has any merit."

"Naw," Nix said incredulously. "That'd be plumb stupid, besides being dangerous. Doesn't she realize that?"

"If she does, she's overlooking it," Chad said bitterly. "She thinks she's helping me. We talked about it as we walked around town. Can I get an advance on my salary?"

Nix looked alertly at him. "What for?"

"I've got to buy a horse, then set out after her."

"Have you got the slightest idea where she went?"

Chad shook his head, his face stricken.

"Then what good will it do to rush all over the country when you don't even know which direction to take?"

"I can't just stand around and wait," Chad said helplessly.

"Did she say anything about how long she would be gone?"

Some of the tautness left Chad's face. "She told Mrs. Tucker she'd be back in about a week."

"Hah," Nix said, his eyes shining. "Then all you can do is to wait for her to return." At the storm rebuilding on Chad's face, he said sternly, "Don't give me any argument. You take off on some crazy tangent and she'll pick that time to return." He saw that he was winning.

"You mean just sit here and wait?"

"It's the only thing you can do," Nix said practically. "I think you've got a pretty level-headed gal. I'd pick her to do what she says about every time."

"Good Lord," Chad groaned. "Do you know how long a week is?"

"The last time I heard, it's seven days," Nix said dryly. He pointed a finger at Chad. "Don't you go swearing at me. I won't stand it. I know how hard it's going to be on you. But you point out one thing you can do."

CHAPTER 16

Nella squirmed uncomfortably on top of a small hill some two hundred yards from the old Ellsworth house. She thought it was a safe distance away, but in a situation like this one could never be sure. Alexander was tethered at the bottom of the hill, another two hundred yards away. Right now, he was glorying in belly-high grass. Nella had pushed the horse and herself as hard as she dared. She was tired, but Alexander showed very few signs of fatigue. If anything, she thought he was sleeker, his eyes brighter. Mr. Tucker had picked his mount well; Alexander had a lot of get-up and go.

She squirmed again and wondered if it was possible that she had picked out an anthill to lie on. She wasn't afraid of them, but she didn't like them crawling over her flesh. Some of those little devils could bite like hell. She saw a red ant crawling over her hand and shook it off. A red ant had poison in its bite, and that bite could make a person howl and jump. She hastily moved to another location, careful to keep low against the skyline. She was sure no one in the house was aware of her presence, but the best way to draw attention was to stand up against the horizon.

She made a hasty inspection of her new location and saw no sign of crawling life. She had crept up the back side of the hill, dragging the canteen of water and the rifle with her. She didn't mind the daylight hours; the night was harder to bear. She didn't know what was crawling on the ground, and there were too many alien sounds she couldn't identify.

She put the glasses to her eyes once more and could see nothing that was particularly interesting. This was her third day out here, and if something didn't break in her favor she wasn't going to make it back to Guthrie when she said she would.

She watched the house until her eyes ached. She lowered the glasses and rubbed her eyes, trying to get the strain out of them. She had spent a lot of her growing-up years in that poor little house, and she didn't remember them with pleasure. The Ellsworths were good enough to her, but her stepsister was another matter. Edith always considered herself superior because she was born an Ellsworth, and that gave her the right to look down at Nella. There had been many heated words between them, and several times the wrangling had developed into hair-pulling and scratching. She smiled wryly as she remembered how many times Mrs. Ellsworth had dashed out of the house to break up the quarrel, then scold them severely. Nella admitted Mrs. Ellsworth had been impartial. She'd given Edith the dickens as much as she had Nella.

She saw a movement near the house and snatched up the glasses. She felt a tremendous disappointment as she saw that it was only Father Ellsworth. She hadn't seen him for several years, and it shocked her to see how he had changed. He was so bent, and his step was so feeble. Nella couldn't understand why he loved this miserable farm so. It had never really produced, but Mr. Ellsworth had clung stubbornly to it. It would kill him one of these days if it hadn't almost done so. Nella looked at her hands. She had put a lot of her youthful energy into this place before she went to Ingalls in search of a job. She watched Ellsworth disappear around the house, and her thoughts went back to work. Ellsworth could thank Bill Doolin for one thing. He could thank him for making it possible to stay on this farm. Bill had been lavish, dispensing his spoils right after he became acquainted with Edith. Ellsworth would do anything for him, including shielding him when he needed it.

Nella pulled another piece of jerky out of her pocket. If she had to eat jerky the rest of her life she swore she would give up eating. She chewed methodically to soften the hard little flake of sun-dried meat. It had a fair taste, she admitted, after the meat was thoroughly softened and the juices flowed. But to Nella it would never take the place of real food.

She resolutely put her attention back on the shabby little house. Oh God, how she wished she could see into that house. Was Doolin inside? Had he reached the Ellsworth farm before Nella did? She hadn't seen him, and she couldn't say. But she knew Edith was here. She had seen her ride in the day before yesterday. That was conclusive proof that Doolin was here. Edith was crazy about the man. She would get to him any time she could. Nella didn't censure her for that feeling. Maybe, in a way, she envied Edith. She wanted the same feeling, but not for a man with criminal tendencies. She wouldn't want her man hiding and sneaking about.

She squirmed again wondering how much longer she would have to stay here. She hadn't had a bath for several days, and she was sure she looked filthy. If she could just catch a glimpse of Doolin, proving he was hiding out at the Ellsworth farm, she could leave. She could get back to Guthrie to fresh clothes and a bath. "Come on, Bill," she muttered.

She held the glasses to her eyes again as Edith came out of the house. The evening sun was going down, and Nella had to squint through the glasses to make sure that was Edith. She wished to God she knew definitely whether or not Doolin was around. Once she had that information, she would take off for Guthrie as fast she could go.

Mr. Ellsworth came hobbling around the house and joined his daughter before he went in. The glasses made them plain to Nella, and she wished she knew what they were talking about. Their faces were angry, looking as though they were quarreling about something. An obscure figure appeared in the doorway, and Nella swung the glasses to him. Her heart skipped a beat, then steadied down into an uneven rhythm. She thought she finally saw Bill Doolin, but he was too deep in the shadows to be sure. Damn it, she prayed.

Move out where I can get a better look at you. He must have called something to Edith, for she turned her head toward the doorway. She gestured wildly, and Nella guessed it could be a warning for him to get back into the house. Whoever it was wasn't taking a woman's orders, for he moved forward a few paces. The fading sunlight played fully on his face, and Nella could be sure it was Doolin. She had never seen him so heavily bearded.

The man and Edith got into a violent argument, then she seized his arm and tried to pull him back into the house. He threw off her arm and moved away. Nella's heart lurched again. The man limped noticeably. She was positive she was looking at Bill Doolin. She flattened out, holding the glasses against the ground. She didn't think they had seen her, but she wanted to take no chances. She was sure she could leave, knowing she had accomplished what she came for. She could go back to Guthrie and tell Chad she knew where Bill Doolin was hiding.

Nella estimated how much daylight was left; she judged it to be a couple of hours until dark. It might be wiser to leave after darkness descended. She didn't know why, but a shiver of apprehension ran through her.

"What are you doing out here?" Edith cried.

Bill Doolin grinned at her. "Being inside is beginning to drive me crazy. Can't I get a breath of fresh air?"

"It might be the most dangerous air you ever tried to breathe," Edith said.

"Aw, come off it," Doolin protested. "How long have I been here?" He figured quickly. "About a week. Nobody strange has been seen around here in that time."

"That might have changed," Edith said quietly.

Doolin stared at her. Edith wasn't a worrier. "What's biting you, Edith?"

"I just caught another flash of light from that hilltop to the east. That's the third one I've seen. Damn it," she almost screamed. "Don't turn and look up there. Do you want whoever it is to know they've been spotted?"

Doolin's face hardened, and he ground his teeth. Were those damned marshals after him again? God, he was so damned weary. The short rest he had had here wasn't enough to fully restore him. "What do you think those flashes of light were?" he asked casually.

"I think they came from field glasses," she answered slowly. "I've been trying to spot who might be using them. So far, I haven't caught a glimpse of them."

"All those flashes come from one spot?" he asked.

Edith nodded.

"That's some relief," Doolin mused. "If they came from a half a dozen different spots, I'd really start to worry. Got any idea who it might be?"

"It might be Nella," she replied, looking him in the eyes. "She messed us up in Ingalls. She helped one of the men you were after." Her face twisted with rancor. Her head hurt every time she remembered the incident. "If she hadn't interfered I'd have taken the other one straight to you. That raid on Ingalls would never have happened."

"Nella?" he protested. "I think you're crazy. I blew up the old Cutter house. Both of them were in it."

"You thought they were," she corrected. "But that's no guarantee."

"Aw, Edith," he grumbled. "You're really getting wild with your guessing."

"Am I?" she challenged. "How many people do you think know where this old farm is? Nella does. She was raised on it. She might have figured out that you're using it to hide out."

His eyes were cold and calculating. He had never known Edith to be far off in her estimation of people. "I didn't get to know Nella very well," he said. "Hell, I didn't do anything to her. In fact, I did her a few favors."

"Including the old Cutter house," Edith said wryly.

He grimaced. "I wasn't after her. I was after the guy she was with. Besides, how did she find out I was behind the dynamiting?"

"Maybe they got out before the dynamite went off," Edith suggested. "They could have been hidden close enough to overhear whatever you said."

Doolin slapped his thigh. "Hell, yes. That's it. The old house caught fire. I thought for sure if the dynamite hadn't gotten those two, the fire would. I didn't bother looking any further."

"That could have been one of your biggest mistakes," Edith said grimly.

Doolin ducked into the house, and Edith followed him. Doolin had picked up his rifle, and his face was mean. "Maybe I can correct that mistake right now."

"Would you shoot her?" Edith asked with sadistic curiosity.

Doolin snapped his fingers. "Like that. I didn't hesitate before. When it comes down to everything, it's either her or me."

"You start up that hill, and she'll see you

coming," Edith pointed out. "She wouldn't come out here unarmed. She can use a gun."

Doolin shook his head. "She won't see me if I slip out of the back door and make a wide circle of that hill. It'll be over before she knows anything about it."

Edith hugged him briefly. "You be careful, Bill," she said against his ear.

"I haven't got this far by being careless," he said, and grinned. "It may take me a couple of hours."

He slipped out of the back door and, by using the shelter of sumac brush, made a wide circle of the hill. He hoped he would see Nella coming down that hill. He didn't actually know that it was Nella spying on him, but he leaned that way.

He climbed the back side of the hill, and swore as he looked at its emptiness. It wasn't a large hilltop, and it didn't take long to search it thoroughly. In some way, she had guessed at his intentions and slipped away. Or she'd learned everything she needed to know, he thought bitterly.

He found evidence that someone had laid here in the mashed-down grass. "It ain't over yet, you bitch," he said savagely.

He went back down the hill, looking for tracks. He found where she had tethered her horse. The horse had been here for quite a while, maybe several days, for a large area of the grass was cropped closely. He found several footprints. They were boot prints, but no man could ever get his foot into a boot that size. "Edith was right again," he muttered. She had called it on the nose when she said Nella had been spying on him. A faint sweat broke out on him, and the night air seemed to turn cold. He was too tired to be put on the run at this time. He needed a long rest, unprodded by some damned marshals.

He stood there for several indecisive moments. There was only one solution open to him. Despite the lead she had, he had to take after her and run her down. He hadn't realized he had clenched his fist until the intensity of his closed fingers put an ache in them. He had missed her at the old Cutter house. He wouldn't miss her this time.

He turned and hurried back toward the farmhouse, despite the pain it put in his crippled foot. He was panting hard when he reached it, and he was sweating heavily.

Edith met him at the door. "What did you find, Bill?"

"I think you were right, Edith, when you guessed it could be Nella. I found out where she tethered her horse, and the imprint of a small boot. It had to be a woman's boot. What other woman than Nella would be interested in what I'm doing?"

She looked beseechingly at him. "What are you going to do, Bill?"

"The only thing I can. Go after her. Shut her up before she has a chance to tell somebody what she found up here. Edith, Dusty is pretty crippled up. I had to use him pretty hard getting here. And he's not fully recovered from that bullet-graze on the rump. Can I take your horse?"

The request put a frown in Edith's eyes. She took so long in answering that it annoyed Doolin. "I didn't expect this from you. If you remember, I bought you that horse. I'm only asking for the loan of it."

"Oh, Bill," Edith cried. "You giving Lady to me is the reason I hesitate. You're pretty heavy for her. And I'm afraid you'll ride her into the ground. You know how you are when you get worked up."

The suspicion cleared from Doolin's face. All those reasons Edith gave him were legitimate. "I promise I won't run her off her hooves."

She searched his face and nodded reluctantly. She came to him and pressed against him for a moment. "Get back as soon as you can, Bill. If you knew how much these few days we've had together without fear of some-body horning —"

He squeezed her hard. "Don't you think that time means something to me? I'll make it as quick as I can. I've got a hunch Nella won't try to ride through the night. If I'm lucky, I may find her asleep."

He said that with such cold ferocity that Edith shivered. His eyes bored into her. "Does what I say bother you, Edith?"

"It does not," she said stoutly. "I won't mourn over whatever happens to her. You know she's never been one of my favorite people. You just get back here quick."

He bent his head to kiss her. "I'll be popping in before you know it. Do you want to go out and supervise Lady's saddling?"

"I do," Edith said crisply. She knew she didn't need to; Bill was an expert horseman, and if anyone could get the best of an animal he could. But he was a big man with solid weight on his bones. Edith shivered as she thought of that weight grinding at Lady during a long trip. She was light-framed for a horse, and not suited to carrying a big man.

Bill cinched up the saddle and grinned at her. "That suit you?"

She colored at his implied criticism. "You know why she's important to me. You just take excellent care of her."

He gave her that appealing, twisted grin. "You know I will, honey. I'd better get going."

"Ma's making some sandwiches for you," Edith said. "She should be out here any minute. Ah," she said with satisfaction. "Here she comes."

Doolin took the bulky bag of sandwiches from the gray-haired old lady. "Ma, you don't know how much I appreciate this." He bent his head to kiss her withered cheek. "Edith, what would be your best guess where she's heading?"

Edith's forehead furrowed in concentration. "I'd say she'll bypass Ingalls. Too many people around there know her too well. That leaves Stillwater and Guthrie. I've got a feeling she did this spying for Nix. His office is in Guthrie. I'd say she's heading for Guthrie."

Doolin nodded in complete agreement. "My figuring exactly. Don't look so worried. I'll catch up with her long before Guthrie comes up."

He put a boot into a stirrup and swung up into the saddle. Edith seemed to literally shrink. Doolin grinned condescendingly at her. "I didn't break her back," he said lightly. "Remember what I promised you. Did you ever know me to break a promise?"

Edith tried to get the anxiety off her face. "You never did to my knowledge, Bill. Just be sure it doesn't happen on this trip."

He waved to both the women, turned the horse, and cantered out.

"You're worried for him, ain't you, Edith?" her mother asked.

"I'm worried about the man and the horse," she said fiercely. "He's too big to be riding Lady."

Her mother patted her hand. "Quit fretting, child. Everything's going to turn out all right. Never been anybody smart enough to corner him yet."

Edith couldn't deny that. But this excursion had a different flavor. She didn't know why, but she had the feeling he would have to go all the way to Guthrie. And that wasn't friendly country, as Ingalls had been.

"The night air's getting a bite to it," her mother said. "I'm going in."

"You go ahead," Edith replied. She was grateful there was a full moon. It meant that she could watch Doolin that much longer.

CHAPTER 17

Doolin started with the area Nella's horse had cropped the grass. A full moon was up early, and Doolin grunted in acknowledgement of its benefit. It would probably be down early, but in the meantime he should have a good general idea of the direction Nella was taking.

It had rained within the last few days, leaving the earth still damp. Doolin picked up a hoofprint almost instantly. He didn't have to get down to investigate it more thoroughly. He could see it from where he sat, and he cocked his head studying it well. There was nothing unusual about the track, except that it was fairly large. Doolin thought he would recognize it when he saw it again.

He set out at a slow pace for two reasons: one, to save Lady from an unnecessary pounding, the other to avoid passing by a horse track that would satisfy him he was still on the trail.

"You'll be sorry you stuck your nose in this, woman," he muttered.

He could quicken Lady's pace, for there was enough damp earth to pick and hold a horse track. It wasn't a normal speed, but Doolin was satisfied. He doubted that Nella was riding at a much greater pace. She wouldn't know that what was behind her was a relentless force that should have sent her fleeing at a breakneck pace.

Doolin judged he had been on the trail a good three hours. Even though the pace hadn't been crushing, he judged it would be wise to dismount and let Lady have a breather. He stopped near another imprint and nodded with satisfaction. He knew that track well now. He had started out well behind Nella, but shortly he would find a place where she turned off for a brief rest. There her eyelids would have grown heavier and heavier until she slipped away into oblivion. His teeth flashed in a cruel grin. Maybe she would never awaken from that sleep. He admitted there was a streak of vindictiveness in him. He never forgot or forgave anybody who crossed him. The sex didn't make any difference.

He tugged on the reins, pulling Lady's head

up. "I know you ain't got enough grass yet, girl. But it'll have to hold you for a while. When we get back, you can eat for days and days." He stepped into the stirrup and swung up. The moon was waning and the light wasn't as brilliant. Doolin scowled. It would make his tracking slower and harder. It wouldn't matter as long as he stopped Nella before she could tell anybody where he was staying. He patted Lady's neck and muttered, "We'll be turning back soon, girl."

Nella was positive no one had seen her watching the Ellsworth place, but still that small apprehension stayed with her. Every now and then, she looked back, and the apprehension subsided a little. She curbed the impulse to put Alexander into a dead run. "Stop it," she admonished herself aloud. "You're just letting nerves work on you." What she said was probably true but, just the same, she would be grateful when Guthrie came into view.

She looked up at the moon. It was beginning to slide down its long descent. She must have been riding for hours, and weariness was beginning to steal over her. She frowned as she debated her course. Should she ride on through the night until she was positive she was out of this alien, unfriendly country? No, she decided. That would be foolish, particularly when it wasn't necessary. She didn't intend to sleep the rest of the night, but a few hours' rest would do her a world of good.

She turned off the road, and rode toward a thick persimmon grove. The trees grew as thick as the hair on a dog's back. This thicket was typical. Nella had to search for an entrance to the grove, and even then the trees brushed her legs on both sides. It wouldn't be as good for Alexander, for grass had to struggle to gain a sparse foothold in this thick shadow.

She slid down from the saddle and said, "Alex, I'm sorry. But it won't do you too much harm. We'll only be here two or three hours." Alexander whinnied softly and bobbed his head as though he understood what she said.

She tied the horse to one of the trees and debated about unsaddling him. She decided against it. With this feeling of uneasiness persisting, she didn't know whether or not she might need him in a hurry.

She sat down with her back against a tree trunk, and the thick gloom of the grove got on her nerves. The rifle leaned against the other side of the tree within close reach of her hand. She didn't want to use it, but if somebody ventured into this grove, she would shoot first and ask questions later. The tension began to slip away from her, and her eyelids grew heavier. It wouldn't hurt to grab a short nap, so she let go.

She didn't know how long she slept, but she came awake with a jerk that sent her head rapping against the trunk. She stared wildly about for a moment before she could place where she was. Relief took over, and the sound she made was half sob, half gasp. Nothing had happened. She looked around, feeling the fear rising within her. She saw nothing moving and heard no alien sound.

The short rest wasn't worth that much for the little good it had done her. She gritted her teeth as she got to her feet and moved about. The returning circulation of blood stuck fiery needles into her legs. She cried out and grabbed a small tree trunk to keep from falling.

She kept moving her legs to force the circulation back. She wouldn't make that mistake again, no matter how weary she was. She didn't know how far she was from Guthrie, but she would keep pushing on until she made the town.

She put another piece of jerky into her mouth and started chewing methodically. Her supply of dried meat was running low. She had to reach Guthrie.

She walked over to Alexander and cradled that long nose briefly in her arms. A person didn't have to know a horse a long time to become devoted to him.

"Let's go, Alex," she whispered. "Next stop home for you."

She mounted, using the strength of her arms to pull herself up. Her legs didn't seem to have the life they once had.

She walked Alexander out of the grove and peered cautiously about her. She couldn't see anything moving. "It's all right, boy," she said, forcing her voice steady. She set Alexander to a stiffer pace, wanting to get back as soon as she could. That eerie feeling remained with her, and she couldn't understand why. She hadn't seen or heard anything alarming.

Doolin missed the tracks turning off into the persimmon grove. He went quite a way before he realized he'd missed them. He swore steadily as he backtracked. All this was eating up time, and he was in a foul mood when he finally picked up the tracks leading to the grove. He found where her horse had been tethered to a tree, and the ground was soft enough to have taken an impression of her buttocks. He glowered at the horse droppings. He couldn't tell how old they were for they no longer steamed. But it couldn't have been too long ago. She had ridden in here to grab a little rest. He wanted to smash a fist into a palm at his feeling of frustration. If he had been just a little faster he might have caught her before she opened her eyes. He didn't know whether or not something actually had awakened her, or whether it was some latent instinct stirring her into motion. He knew one thing for certain. They were several miles closer to Guthrie. His time for getting at her was growing shorter. He was swearing fluently as he rode out of the grove. He had to go back to the tedious task of tracking her again.

CHAPTER 18

Doolin's swearing grew more passionate as he saw that this country hadn't known as much rain as the country where he'd started his chase. The footprints were gone. While her passage might have raised some dust he couldn't count on it as he did on the hoofprints. "She's going to Guthrie," he muttered to himself. Once he had determined her direction, he could ride faster and harder. He still couldn't say how many miles remained before Guthrie came into view, but it was still a good piece. He groaned as he thought of Nella reaching Guthrie. She would babble her guts out, and that would point the marshals straight at the Ellsworth farm. He debated his course of action: abandon his chase and turn back, or go on. Damn it, he had known a sort of peace on the farm, and Edith had been with him.

Running and hiding was a hell of a life for a man. He wouldn't let go of that peace, not yet. As long as Nella hadn't reached Guthrie there was still hope he could catch up with her before she entered town. At least he could save time by not having to slow down to look for more hoofprints. Once her destination was determined he could throw everything else aside and just ride hard. He grimaced as he thought of how Edith would raise hell when he brought back a worn-out Lady, but it couldn't be helped. The sun was up full, and the heat of the day was building up. Could Lady last another day? He judged it would take that long before Guthrie came into view. He just didn't know. He reached over and patted the mare's sweaty neck. "You're doing just fine, girl," he muttered. How much distance did Nella have on him? Doolin wished to God that he knew.

Nella judged she should be in Guthrie about nightfall. She was so tired she ached in every bone, and the feeling of apprehension hadn't lessened. But Alexander hadn't faltered. His hide was beginning to glisten with sweat, but he was a stout-hearted horse with a great deal of bottom in him. She had no worry about him quitting. Her greater worry was if she could last until Guthrie.

At every high point on the road, Nella would look back. She saw nothing. Was her imagination playing her fearful tricks? She hoped so. She was out of jerky and almost out of water. God, she was so tired and hungry, and she didn't dare attempt to do anything about either condition. She knew that if she ever got off Alexander to rest she might not be able to get back on him. She wasn't sorry she had gone on this excursion — she knew where Bill Doolin was — but she did wish it was well behind her. She also wished there was some way to get the miles to fall behind her faster.

By mid-afternoon she was almost faint, and if it weren't for the horn to cling to she thought she might fall out of the saddle. She tried to keep track of Alexander's steps, counting them as he took them, but she lost count around fifty.

"Gal," she said aloud, needing the sound of a human voice to bolster her. "You're getting giddy."

She still remembered, every time she reached a high spot, to glance behind her. Seeing no horseman encouraged her. "What would you do if there was one?" she asked herself practically. A touch of the gamin was in her smile. "You'd just have to race whoever it was back to Guthrie."

The sun was beginning its descent when she felt a tremendous disappointment. She wasn't going to reach Guthrie before dark.

This country was beginning to look more familiar to her with every step the horse took. She wasn't more than a few miles out of Guthrie, and it didn't make any difference how late she arrived. The shadows were lengthening when she saw the first house on the outskirts of Guthrie. Even as she watched, a light went on in the house. She didn't expect to see very many people on the streets. This was the supper hour, or close to it. She could have screamed her jubilation. She was going to make it.

She looked back more out of habit than need, and her heart jumped into her throat. There was a horseman behind her, less than a mile behind.

Her heels drummed frantically on Alexander's flanks as she tried to get more speed out of him. She couldn't definitely say who the rider was, but an instinct told her who it was. That could be nobody else but Bill Doolin, and he was flogging his mount, for she caught the motion of his arm as it rose and fell.

Oh God, to come so close and then not make it. Her lips were stretched painfully over her teeth, and she sobbed for breath. If she could get to Mrs. Tucker's boarding house, she would be all right, for it wouldn't take her longer than a moment to get inside. She didn't think Doolin would dare to try and break into the house.

She turned a corner, and here was the alley that passed Alexander's shed. "Just a little farther, boy," she begged. "Don't falter now."

She couldn't believe her eyes. Was she losing her mind? Somebody stood before the shed, and she was sure it was a man. That couldn't be Doolin. It was impossible for him to have made up the distance between them.

Her vision cleared, and she sobbed her relief. Now she was sure she wasn't imagining things. That tall, lanky figure could belong to nobody else but Chad Grimes.

He sprang forward and seized Alexander's bridle. Nella slid to the ground, and she doubted she could stand. "Oh, Chad," she cried, making no attempt to disguise the relief in her voice. "Am I glad to see you."

His face didn't soften. "Where in the hell have you been? I've been out to this shed four or five times a day, looking for you."

She forgave him his anger. That was based on worry. "Hold me, Chad, before I fall down." She was so light-headed she was sure she would be babbling hysterically in a moment.

She staggered to him, and his arms went about her. "Damn you, Nella. Where have you been?"

She was close to hysteria, and it showed in her shaky laughter. "I thought I knew where Bill Doolin could be hiding. I went to check it out. I was right, Chad. I saw him. I think he saw me, or in some way knew that I'd been spying on him. I think he's right behind me. I saw a horseman coming after me, and he was beating his horse. Oh Chad, get me inside."

Her words brought a stunned look to his face, and for a moment he couldn't believe what he was hearing. "Aw, Nella, you're imagining things. Doolin wouldn't dare ride into Guthrie."

He heard the sharp, crashing report of rifle, its echoes slamming from building to building. Nella gave a faint, choked cry, her eyes rolled up into her head and she slumped in his arms. The surprise was so devastating that Chad wasn't prepared to hold her, and she slid from his arms to the ground. His head whipped to the mouth of the alley about a hundred yards away. In the gathering darkness, he heard the sound of a man running, and it had an odd sound, as though the man ran limpingly. . . . A moment later, he heard the pound of a horse's hooves.

Chad wanted to go after the assassin, but he couldn't. Nella was crumpled up at his feet.

CHAPTER 19

The sound of the shot had whipped Chad's head around toward the mouth of the alley. He was in time to see a vague, shadowy figure turn and run awkwardly away. Chad would say the awkward run was the result of a lame foot, but he wasn't close enough to be sure.

The motionless figure at his feet held him chained here, and he dropped to his knees beside her. She was breathing, but it was shallow and labored. "Nella, Nella," he cried out, but she made no response. Instinctively, Chad knew he hadn't better try to turn or lift her. Even to his untrained eye, she was badly hurt.

He looked around helplessly. He had never felt so alone, so desperate in his life.

The sound of the shot must have reached Mrs. Tucker, for she came running out of her rear door. She saw Chad kneeling over Nella, but at the moment she was too distraught to think clearly. "Chad," she cried. "I thought I heard a shot."

"You did," he said grimly. "Nella just got back. Somebody followed her. He just gunned her down. I couldn't go after him. I had to stay with Nella."

"Did you know him?" Mrs. Tucker whimpered.

"I think I do," Chad said in a tight-lipped voice.

"Is Nella dead?" Mrs. Tucker was very close to hysterics.

"Not yet. When I listened a moment ago, she was still breathing. Mrs. Tucker, will you go and get a doctor? Somebody has to stay here." His voice cracked and threatened to break. "And hurry," he begged.

Mrs. Tucker couldn't have been gone very long, but to Chad it seemed like an eternity. He kept listening for the returning sound of footsteps, and when it didn't come he wanted to bawl. He had to keep an iron control on his nerves, or he would shatter like a dropped china dish.

He finally heard footsteps coming, and Mrs. Tucker's voice verified it, "Over here, doctor. She's been shot. Chad, this is Dr. Jones."

Chad nodded impatiently. He didn't care

who she had found; he just wanted medical attention for Nella. "What do you think, Doctor?"

"I just got here," Jones replied. "Give me time to make my examination," he finished dryly.

He knelt beside the unconscious woman and swore at the poor light. "You say she was shot?"

"Yes," Chad snapped. Oh God, wouldn't this man get on with it? "She was facing that way." He indicated where Nella had been standing. "I hadn't seen her for several days. I was hugging her when the shot sounded. She crumpled and slid out of my arms. I didn't dare move her."

"Wise," Jones approved. He put his ear close to Nella's lips. "Still breathing, though it's faint. I'll need your help in turning her over."

"Is that wise?" Chad asked worriedly.

"Didn't you say her back was turned toward the mouth of the alley?" Jones asked brusquely. "How will I know where the wound is unless I look?"

Chad nodded sheepishly. That made sense. "You tell me what you want."

"Take her feet. I'll take her shoulders. We'll try to turn her over without further shock to her."

That was one of the hardest jobs Chad ever attempted. The tension gripped him so hard he wanted to yell against it. Come on, he admonished himself. You're not going to be any good to her if you go all to pieces.

He waited until Jones said, "Now. And gently."

Chad lifted Nella's legs and turned her. He breathed hard. She seemed so frail, so light and helpless. He worked with Jones, trying to match his every motion. At any moment he expected Nella to cry out in protest against the handling. Instinctively, he knew that she was badly hurt, and he hurt in sympathy.

They got Nella turned over, and Jones said, "Ah."

The flat word expressed everything, for the spreading blood was obvious, even in the dim light. A glistening, moist spot covered the small of Nella's back.

"Is it bad?" Chad asked, fighting to keep his voice from breaking.

Jones looked at him witheringly. "Bad enough, I'd say. That bleeding's got to be stopped."

"Then do it," Chad said harshly.

The annoyance was more pronounced in Jones's voice. "Here?" he asked. "I've got to get her to more adequate facilities."

"Where's that going to be?" Chad cried.

"In my office," Jones snapped. "It's less than a block from here." He sensed the outraged protest in Chad's manner, and he asked, "Or do you want her to lie here and bleed to death?"

A block seemed an interminable distance, and Chad wanted to cry. "Can we get her to your office?" he asked. His voice was breaking on him.

"We've got to," Jones said crisply. He bent to take Nella's shoulders again. "Take her legs. For God's sake, man, match your steps with mine. Move like you're walking on eggs."

Chad had never felt more helpless. He was a taller man, and he imagined his steps were longer.

"Can I help?" Mrs. Tucker asked. She sounded far more composed than Chad did.

"Move along beside us," Jones instructed her. "Maybe you can help us carry her weight."

"Wouldn't a stretcher do better?" Mrs. Tucker asked practically.

Jones frowned at her. "There'd be the lost time of going after one and getting it here. Time's my enemy now."

Mine, too, Chad thought as he bent in unison. Rage built up inside him as he lifted his part of the weight. He had so much anger at the man who was responsible for this. I'll find him, Nella, he promised her silently.

Chad had never known a trip so long or so arduous. He was limp from exhaustion when Jones finally said, "In here," indicating a door of a building just ahead. Chad could have sobbed with relief as he helped carry Nella inside. His legs ached from matching Jones's steps. Mrs. Tucker had never uttered a complaint as she moved along with them.

They stepped inside Jones's office, but the chore wasn't over yet. "In the back room," Jones said. It had been a wearing trip on him, too, for his face was a mask of strain. He was an average-sized man with the beginning of a paunch. He must have been in his fifties, and the carrying had worn on him. His face was gray, his eyes glassy. "I've got a table back there," he went on, beginning to puff. He glanced at Chad, and his eyes sharpened. "Don't falter now, man."

Chad wanted to howl at him. "I'm not faltering now," he snapped.

"Good," Jones said approvingly. "I want her placed on the table, face down."

He jerked his head at Mrs. Tucker, and she was good at anticipating his orders. She let go of Nella and hurried to the door, opening it, then standing as far out of the way as she could.

"Good woman," Jones grunted.

They laid Nella face down on the bleak table, and Jones lit a lamp and moved it close to the table. The radiance illuminated the massive blood stain on Nella's back. Chad closed his eyes and weaved.

Jones caught the signs. "Wait outside, please." He raised a hand, stopping Chad's objection. "It's plain to see you haven't been around gunshot wounds before."

"I feel faint," Chad confessed. "She means so much to me."

"It always hits a person harder that way," Jones commented. "Go on. Get out. The bullet is probably still in her back. It has to be taken out." He smiled whimsically. "I don't think you could stand seeing it removed."

Chad's mouth was suddenly dry, and his stomach felt queasy. Jones was right in his estimate of him, but Chad didn't like his weakness being pointed out. "You've done it before?"

"Many times," Jones assured him. "It's always harder when you care for the person involved," he said in a more kindly tone.

"Can you save her?"

"That remains to be seen." The doctor's authoritative manner had returned. "Mrs. Tucker, can you assist me?"

"Yes," she answered promptly. "If

you tell me what to do."

"I'll tell you," Jones assured her. "I'll probably be barking at you before this is over." He removed his coat, rolled up his sleeves, and glanced at Chad. "What are you waiting for?"

Chad turned and scurried out of the room. His knees felt as though they were going to dump him on the floor. The last thing he saw before he left the room was Jones pouring water into a pan.

Chad seated himself in a hard chair in the outer office. God, he felt so alone. He had no idea of how long he would have to wait, but something told him it would be the longest, hardest time he had ever spent.

He leaned his head back against the wall, closed his eyes, and tried to empty his head of all thoughts, but his mind wouldn't cooperate. He heard every little sound: the barking of a dog outdoors, the ticking of a clock on the wall, the buzzing of a fly as it flew across the room. God, this kind of waiting was pure misery. He had never been a religious man, and now he wished he had been one. Maybe he would have had someone to turn to with his desperate entreaty.

He didn't know how long he sat there, but it must have been forever. The opening of that inner door jerked him out of his stupor. He jumped to his feet as Mrs. Tucker came into the office.

"Mrs. Tucker, how did it go? Is Nella all right?"

She didn't look as though a drop of blood remained in her face. "It was horrible," she whispered. "I've got to sit down before I fall down."

He led her to the chair he had just vacated and helped her sit down. "Did she come through all right?" he insisted.

She shuddered, as though shaking away some horrible vision. "The doctor said she was tough. She had to be to withstand all that cutting. . . ." Tears filled her eyes, and she buried her face in her hands.

Chad let her cry uninterruptedly for a few moments, then he shook her gently. He had to know about Nella.

"Mrs. Tucker," he said, his voice sterner. "I've got to know."

She raised her head. Tears glistened on her cheeks. "Of course you do. Dr. Jones will be out in a moment or so. I'd rather he tell you all about it."

Chad's heart felt heavier than a stone. Was what she said a way of preparing him for some dreadful news? Oh God; he wanted to rave and rant. He wanted to smash his fist into something.

242

Jones came out a few moments later, and he gave Chad a bleak grin. "Looks like you've been suffering," he commented.

Chad slashed his palm through the air. It wasn't important about him. The only important thing was how Nella was doing. "Doc, how is she?"

Jones had taken time to wash his hands, but Chad could see traces of blood, Nella's blood. "She came through as well as could be expected," he said brusquely. He grinned bleakly at Mrs. Tucker. "I was afraid I was going to lose my nurse. But she did just fine."

Chad wanted to grab and shake the truth out of him. "Doctor, is she going to make it?"

Jones regarded him gravely. "The bullet was deep. I had to cut pretty far to get at it," He reached into his pocket and pulled out a misshapen slug. "Here it is. I'd say it's a Winchester."

Chad wanted to curse him with all the passion in his being. Was Jones deliberately avoiding telling Chad what he wanted so frantically to hear? "Doc," he said imploringly.

Jones tried to hand Chad the slug, and Chad shook his head. Jones shrugged. "Thought you might want to keep it. The reason I didn't follow Mrs. Tucker out immediately is that I had to do some final bandaging. Then I gave her a sedative. She's sleeping now." He shook his head in amazement. "For such a slip of a girl, she's tough."

Chad's hands opened and closed. "Doc," he said, and there was a threat in the single word.

Jones chuckled. "I'd say she's got a fifty-fifty chance of pulling through."

The tension drained out of Chad, leaving him empty. He was very close to tears. He could feel them stinging in his eyes. "Can I see her now?" he babbled.

Jones gave him a reproving look. "My God, man. She's just come through a very tough operation. That bullet hit her in the back just six inches from her heart. Just six inches." His tone had that wondering note again. "If it had been that six inches closer nobody could have done anything for her."

"Does that mean I can't see her?" Chad asked in a disappointed voice.

"Have you heard anything I've said?" Jones asked in disgust. "She'll be out for hours. Maybe even days. Rest is the best thing for her right now." He turned his head toward Mrs. Tucker. "Mrs. Tucker, you go on home. You can compliment yourself on a fine job. I couldn't have done it without your help."

Mrs. Tucker flushed and beamed with pleasure. "I'd be glad to stay, Doctor. Something might come up so that you might need me."

He gently shook his head. "I won't, Mrs. Tucker. I'll be here. I wouldn't dare leave her until I'm sure she's on the road to recovery. You look exhausted. Go on now. Get on home."

He fixed those stern eyes on Chad. "You too. There's nothing you can do."

Chad stubbornly shook his head. "I'm staying, damn it," he said, his voice rising. "Do you think I could leave now?"

Jones studied him a long moment. "Do as you want," he said. A fleeting grin touched his face. "You will anyway. Now, if you'll excuse me, I've got to look in on Nella."

He disappeared into that back room, and the door closed behind him.

"Chad, come with me," Mrs. Tucker implored. "You heard what the doctor said."

"No," Chad said fiercely. "I've got to stay."

Mrs. Tucker looked at him a long moment, then sighed. "I guess you do." She went out, and the door closed behind her.

Chad settled back into the chair. That brutal waiting would start all over, but it would be better this time. Renewed hope flooded him. He didn't like the odds Jones had given Nella, but she had made it so far. He had to believe she would make it all the way.

CHAPTER 20

Jones's light touch awakened Chad. His eyes flew open, and he stared groggily about him. For a moment, he couldn't place where he was. It was broad daylight, and he realized he had fallen asleep in that uncomfortable chair. Realization hit him, and he jumped to his feet. Jones had come out here to give him some bad news.

"She's worse. Nella's . . ." Chad faltered and couldn't say the dread word.

Jones wearily shook his head. "I despair of the pessimism in human nature. Why do you have to jump to the worst conclusion? No, she's no worse. No better either. But her pulse remains strong. That gives me every hope."

Chad looked at the drawn face, at the utter weariness in the eyes. "You didn't sleep at all," he cried.

Jones smiled wanly. "I may have dozed off a time or two. It's no substitute for a decent night's rest. I'm going across the street for a cup of coffee. Care to come with me?"

Chad shook his head. "Somebody should stay with her."

"Not necessary," Jones said brusquely. "We won't be gone that long." As the stubbornness remained in Chad's face, he said crossly, "Do you think I'd risk anything that could bring harm to her?"

Chad's stubbornness faded. "I guess not," he muttered. He took a step, and yelped as savage little needles pierced his legs.

Jones chuckled and said, "Returning circulation. That chair is hardly a fit place to sleep."

Chad agreed with him heartily. Those sharp stabs of agony hit him every step, and his neck was stiff. "I'd have been smarter to sleep on the floor," he grumbled. "But I was positive I wouldn't fall asleep."

Jones nodded. "When a person has that much on his mind he swears the body no longer has any demands on him. But in the long run the body wins."

Chad was moving easier by the time they crossed the street and entered the restaurant. The sign on the window proclaimed "Ma's Place."

"Good place to eat?" Chad asked.

"Let's say convenient," Jones said dryly. "A good restaurant is a rarity in this town."

It was early in the morning, and Chad and Jones were the only customers in the place. Ma was a tired-looking woman who moved as though her feet hurt her.

"What'll you have, Doctor?" she asked crossly.

"Ah," Jones said knowingly. "Somebody else didn't sleep too well last night. Is the coffee ready?"

Her tone didn't lighten. "It's ready," she snapped. "I swear I'll never get used to getting up early. A body could do very well if only it didn't have to stir around to make a living." She cut her eyes at Chad. "How about you, youngun?"

"Coffee, and . . ." Chad hesitated. He looked at Jones for assistance. His belly was empty. He needed more than just coffee.

Jones guessed at his predicament. "I'd say pancakes. They'll fill you. Nobody can go very far off in ordering them."

Chad's hope rose as he sipped at his coffee. It was hot and strong, but it was still good. Maybe Jones was wrong in his evaluation of the food here.

Ma served him the pancakes, and Chad's face

fell at the first forkful.

Jones grinned at his expression. "It'll fill you. That's all you eat for anyway, isn't it?"

"If that's true I'll never look forward to another meal." He poured more syrup on them to disguise the raw taste.

Even with the added syrup, he couldn't get all the pancakes down. He groaned silently as he thought of the excellent food he had eaten at Mrs. Tucker's.

He didn't comment until they got outside. "I don't think that woman knows how to cook," he said bitterly.

"Probably not," Jones said lightly. "She's struggling to hold on."

"But you picked her place," Chad accused him.

"Only for its convenience," Jones defended himself. "It's quick and close. You notice I didn't order anything but coffee."

Chad shook his head. "If she's having trouble making it it wouldn't surprise me."

"That place has already changed hands three times this year," Jones said. "And now Ma." His expression was thoughtful. "I wonder if a place like that gets an aura of failure that carries over to the next owner."

"Could be," Chad grunted. He followed Jones into his office. "I know Nella isn't awake.

But could I just look in on her for a moment?"

Jones frowned, then nodded. "Yes, but just look in. Don't try to go into the room." He opened the door, then stepped inside for Chad to look in.

Nella was covered with several blankets, and their bulk dwarfed her. Her eyes were closed, and Chad couldn't see any sign of her breathing.

He started to ask Jones about it, but Jones had already stepped into the room for a closer look at his patient. Chad knew better than to attempt to follow him.

He had another bad time of waiting for Jones to return, though it wasn't as long as other times he had waited. He waited until Jones closed the door of the room. "Is she worse, Doc?" he asked anxiously.

Jones snorted. "Have you always been a fretter? Didn't you see the color in her face? It gets better with each passing hour. Her pulse was stronger too."

"But her eyes were closed," Chad objected. "She didn't look that good to me."

Jones grinned sardonically. "Then you should be glad I'm her doctor and not you. She hasn't come out of the sedative yet. You're forgetting she suffered a tremendous shock to her system. She may not come out of it today, or even tomorrow."

"Oh God," Chad moaned.

"That kind of rest is good for her," Jones said. "That's nature's way of healing. Do you want me to go in there and try to shake her into consciousness?" he asked sarcastically.

"You know I didn't mean that," Chad said heatedly.

"Go back to Mrs. Tucker's and get some proper sleep," Jones suggested. "It'd be easier on the two of us."

"No way." Chad shook his head determinedly. "I've got to be here when she comes to."

Jones threw up his hands in disgust. "God deliver me from having patients like you." He disappeared into the rear room and came back with his arms filled with blankets and pillows. "As long as you insist on staying," he growled, "this might make it a little more comfortable for you."

"I appreciate this," Chad said solemnly. He started to say he wouldn't need them, that he had no intention of going to sleep again, then held the words. The same vow had been in his head before he fell asleep last night.

He made a pallet of two of the blankets and stretched out on them. The blankets softened the hard floor. God, this was luxury. Before a second thought came to mind, he was asleep.

He had no idea of how long he had slept, but he had the feeling it was quite a stretch.

A rough hand gripped his shoulder and unceremoniously shook him awake. Chad's eyes popped open, and he glared at the offender. For a moment, he didn't recognize Nix, and he said in anger, "What the hell?"

Nix squatted down beside him. "Whoa," he said calmly. "It's mid-afternoon. Time for you to be awake anyway. I stopped by Mrs. Tucker's to talk to you. She told me what happened last night and said you'd probably still be here. How bad is Nella?"

"I don't know," Chad said miserably. "The last time I asked the doctor she was still unconscious." He sat up and tried to knuckle the grains out of his eyes.

"You been asleep here all that time?" Nix asked incredulously.

"I was up and had breakfast," Chad said defensively. He started to say something else, and Jones came out of the rear room. "How is she, Doc?" Chad cried.

"Still unconscious," Jones said cheerfully. "But getting stronger. I expect her to come to before the day is out. Marshal," he begged, "take him with you. I can't get rid of him."

Nix nodded. "I want to talk to him anyway.

Chad, don't you want something to eat?"

Chad's belly growled, and he said, "I sure could use something." He looked at Jones and said, "I'll be back."

Jones sighed. "I knew that."

Chad walked outdoors with Nix. "There's a restaurant across the street," he suggested.

Nix snorted. "I tried Ma's just once. That was enough. There's a better restaurant not three blocks away." At Chad's hesitation, he said firmly, "You won't be needed. The doctor's with her."

Chad gave in reluctantly and accompanied Nix to the place he recommended. He noticed the difference the moment he stepped into the new restaurant. It was cleaner, and the rank smell of grease wasn't in the air. "What do you suggest?" he asked.

"Ham and eggs," Nix answered promptly. "It takes a bad cook to do much to them."

"Ma could," Chad said positively. He ordered four fried eggs and a big slab of ham. "Add a portion of fried potatoes," he said.

His hunger grew as he waited for the food to be prepared. He took a cautious sip of his coffee and murmured, "Ah. That tastes like coffee."

Nix grinned, then his face sobered. "It's been a bad time for you hasn't it?"

"The worst," Chad said flatly. He closed his eyes, remembering the anxious hours of waiting.

"Any idea of who did it?" Nix asked softly.

"I think it was Bill Doolin."

Nix's eyes rounded. "Are you imagining things?"

"I was there when Nella got back," Chad said. "She told me she'd seen Doolin, and she thought he might be following her. That murdering bastard got her in the back. She slid right out of my arms."

"That all you've got to go on?" Nix asked impatiently.

"It was almost dark, but I caught a glimpse of him," Chad growled. "He was running away. He was limping. I couldn't leave her," he finished.

"Sure you couldn't," Nix agreed.

The woman brought the food then, and she set the steaming plates before the men. "I hope you like it, Marshal."

"I always have, Nelly," he said, and smiled.

The food was good. Chad hadn't realized how empty he was until he tasted palatable food. He ate like a long-starved wolf and, until the meal was finished, not a word was exchanged between them.

Chad cleaned up his plate and said regretfully, "I should've ordered a couple more eggs."

"My God," Nix said in astonishment. "You already ate more than two men. I only ordered half of what you did."

Unabashed, Chad grinned. "I'm still a growing boy." He pulled some coins out of his pocket and laid them on the counter. "Fine meal, ma'am."

She beamed all over her face, her pleasure showing. That was also different from the first restaurant. Chad hadn't had anything to compliment the owner about.

As they walked back to Jones's office, Chad said, "God, I hope she comes out of it."

Nix nodded. "Me too. The fact that she's hung on this long is all in her favor. She must be one tough gal."

"Doc said about the same thing."

Jones was waiting for them when they returned, and he seemed impatient. "I thought you'd never return."

A giant hand squeezed Chad's heart until he thought he would black out. "Something's happened to Nella," he said hoarsely.

Jones looked at Nix and shook his head. "Worst worrier I ever knew. If something happened, why couldn't it be good?"

Chad was owl-eyed, "You mean it's all to the good?"

Jones nodded solemnly. "She came to just a couple of minutes ago. For an instant, she didn't know what had happened to her, then it came back; she remembered everything. She wanted to see you. I told her you'd be back shortly."

"Can I see her?" Chad asked eagerly.

Jones frowned as he made a decision. "No longer than a couple of minutes. She's awfully weak, and she'll probably slip back into sleep at any moment. Right now, I want her to sleep all she can."

"I won't stay long," Chad promised.

"I know you won't," Jones said sternly. "Because I'll be right there to jerk you out of that room."

He opened the door, and Chad literally tip-toed in.

Her eyes were opened, and she watched him cross the room. My God, he hadn't realized how beautiful those eyes were.

"Hello, Nella," he whispered. He bent over and brushed her forehead with his lips. "How do you feel?"

"Tired," she said in a faint voice. "How did I get here?"

"Dr. Jones, Mrs. Tucker, and I carried you

here. Do you remember being shot?"

Her forehead creased. "I remember something hitting my back, and the awful pain. Then everything went black."

"You don't know how scared I was, Nella. Dr. Jones got the bullet out. He saved your life."

She tried to smile, and the attempt was weak. "I'm grateful to him."

Her eyes seemed to grow heavy, and she had to struggle with her next sentence. "It was Doolin, wasn't it?"

Chad had to bend closer to hear that faint voice. "I think it was. Don't try to talk about it now."

Her eyes were almost closed. "I hope you find him. He's a vicious man, Chad."

Chad nodded. "I'll find him. When I'm sure you're fully recovered —" He stopped. He had no listener; Nella's eyes were closed.

"Doc," he said, his face frantic. "She went to sleep right while I was talking to her."

Jones made a brief examination. "Natural. Just that little effort exhausted her. Her pulse is strong. I told you she needed all the rest she could get." He pushed Chad toward the door as he talked. "Right now your talking to her is through. Maybe you can talk to her again when she awakens."

Chad felt a surge of rebellion. Nella had information that he needed badly. "How long will that be?"

Jones shrugged in irritation. "Who knows?"

"I'm going to stay here until she comes to," Chad stated.

"I expected you to," Jones said dryly.

Chad joined Nix in the outer room. "I talked to her, Evett. She's stronger. She's going to recover fully. Isn't she?" he challenged Jones.

Jones sighed. What a gadfly this man was. "She will, if there's no complication." At the frown on Chad's face, he said hastily, "I see no reason why there should be."

Nix drew Chad to one side. "Did she tell you where she saw Doolin?" Nix asked.

"She didn't have time before she drifted off to sleep. Doc said that was normal. She needs all the sleep she can get."

"Then you still don't know anything?"

"I will," Chad said grimly. "I'm going to kill Doolin. If anybody needs killing, he's the one."

"I'm in favor of that," Nix said crisply. "But, with the little information you have, a clever lawyer could get him off. No, I think he's earned a bullet between the eyes. Shooting a girl in the back . . ." He shook his head and didn't finish. He was silent a moment, then asked, "What do you plan to do, Chad?"

"I intend to be here when she wakes up again," Chad replied.

Nix nodded. "I'll be here too. I want to ask her some questions."

Jones came up in time to overhear the conversation. "If you think you're going to grill that girl, forget it," he said savagely.

Nix looked astounded at Chad. "What set him off?"

"I guess he's pretty well worn out. He's set himself up as some kind of a protector for Nella."

Jones's eyes flashed. "She may not wake up the whole night."

Chad's jaw jutted forward. "I'm staying."

"I thought you would," Jones said in utter disgust. He was swearing softly as he stalked out of the room.

"A tough customer," Nix commented.

"I guess that quality pulled Nella through," Chad said. "I can't get sore at him, no matter what he does."

CHAPTER 21

At the end of a couple of hours, Nix was fidgeting. "It don't look like she's going to wake up soon," he commented.

Chad's eyes were unfriendly. "Do you want me to go in there and wake her up?"

"I didn't say that," Nix protested.

"No, but you meant it," Chad said shortly.

Nix stood, and his face was injured. "You forget I've got an office to run."

Chad's nerves were showing raw ends. "Nobody's holding you here." Nix didn't appreciate the fact that Nella was fighting for her life.

Nix sighed. "You get an idea in your head, and there's no room for anything else."

"What's that mean?" Chad asked hotly.

"Forget it." An edge had appeared in Nix's voice. "I'll be back in a little while."

"Do that," Chad said. Right now, he didn't care if he saw Nix again or not.

Jones came in a few moments later, and he had a woman with him. "Chad, this is Mrs. Moore. She's a competent nurse. I've been trying to get her for the past several weeks, but she had some personal matters to take care of. Now maybe I can get some decent sleep."

Chad nodded gravely. Lord knew Jones deserved that. It had been a long stretch since Jones had known several uninterrupted hours. A man could only go so far on a wink here and a wink there before everything fell in on him.

"Mrs. Moore," Jones said. "I don't expect Nella to awaken for several hours. There won't really be anything for you to do. Just keep a close eye on her. If she should worsen, and I don't expect that, get in touch with me immediately. This is Chad, her young man. He's been understandably worried about Nella's condition. When Nella does wake I expect she'll be starved."

Mrs. Moore had a bright, intelligent face. "What should I feed her, Doctor?"

"Oh, something light. I'd suggest soup. It's nourishing and warmth-giving. I've got several cans in that cupboard over there. Maybe in the morning she can have something more solid."

Mrs. Moore nodded. "I'll take care of everything Doctor. Now you get out of here."

She didn't speak until the door closed behind Jones. "Poor man," she murmured. "He's worn out."

"I can vouch for that," Chad said. "He didn't think of leaving Nella until he was sure she was out of danger."

Mrs. Moore surveyed him with bright, interested eyes. "Have you been here all that time too?"

Chad nodded. "That's not quite honest. I slept some of that time."

"She means a lot to you, doesn't she?"

Chad smiled. "I never knew how much until I saw how she was fighting for her life. I owe Dr. Jones a debt I'll never be able to repay."

Her eyes twinkled. "He won't expect that kind of payment. Now I'd better look in on my patient."

She was gone only a few seconds. When she returned she said. "Still sleeping peacefully. She looks so helpless. I can understand your feeling for her."

Chad felt color heating his face, but he couldn't deny the truth. "You'll let me know when she wakes up," he begged.

"You know it," Mrs. Moore said promptly. She settled down beside him. It was good to have somebody like her to talk to. It was different with Nix. Nix's interest was only in what information he could get out of Nella. He'll never get that information, Chad vowed.

Time passed pleasantly enough. Chad was surprised to see how many hours had slipped off the clock. Mrs. Moore was never lax in her duty to her patient. Every now and then, she excused herself and entered the rear room. Each time she returned and she shook her head. It only meant that Nella was still sleeping.

It was nearing midnight when Mrs. Moore reentered the room. When she came out she didn't shake her head at Chad. She went straight to the cupboard, took out a can, opened it and poured the contents into a pan. Then she busied herself with building a fire in the small stove.

Chad watched her, comprehension slowly dawning. "She's awake," he cried.

"Yes," Mrs. Moore said simply. "Do you know something? She woke up hungry. I'll have a bowl of soup ready in a few minutes."

"Could I see her?" Chad asked. "I promise I'll leave the moment you bring in the soup."

"I don't see why that isn't possible," Mrs. Moore said after a moment's reflection.

Chad tip-toed into the room. A lamp was on, and its radiance reflected in the shine of her eyes. "You slept long enough," he said gruffly.

"What time is it, Chad?"

"Almost midnight."

"Have you been out there all that time?" At Chad's nod, she murmured, "Poor Chad."

He shook his head. "I wasn't the one who was hurt. How do you feel?"

"Hungry," she answered.

He gestured impatiently. "I guessed that. Do you hurt?"

She smiled at him, and it was much stronger. "Only when I try to walk."

His delight at her remark was obvious. "If you ain't the one," he said, and chuckled. "Of all the damned fool things to do."

"I did it for you, Chad," she said in a small voice. "I felt you were in danger as long as Doolin was alive."

"You actually saw him?" he asked in wonder.

She nodded. "I did. Through the field glasses I took with me."

"How close were you to him?" Maybe this was only her over-inventive imagination working.

"You don't believe me?" she said indignantly. "I thought he might be at the old Ellsworth farm northwest of Ingalls. Edith and I were raised there. I rode there to see if Bill would be coming around. I was right." She couldn't disguise the small triumph in her voice. "He'd do anything to get to Edith. There's a small hill east of the farmhouse. I lay out there to watch for him. It took me three days to catch a glimpse of him, but he was there all right. He had grown a beard, so at first I didn't know him."

"What made you stick so long?" Chad asked, half angry.

"Because Edith was there. I saw her the first day. I just knew Bill would get to her. There's always been a strong bond between them."

"If you were well I'd spank you," he growled. "Taking chances like that."

"It wasn't such a big chance."

"He followed you back to Guthrie, didn't he?"

A frown touched her face. "Yes, he did. How did he find out I was spying on him?"

Chad shook his head; he couldn't answer that. Before he could say anything else, Jones came in with Mrs. Moore, who carried a bowl of soup.

"I thought I'd find you in here," Jones said crossly. "I didn't give Mrs. Moore complete instructions about keeping you out."

"Your sleep didn't seem to do you much good," Chad said, and grinned.

"I didn't get as much as I wanted. Now get

out of here. I'd like to check her wound. Then Mrs. Moore wants to feed her." His face firmed at the argument forming in Chad's face. "I mean it, Chad. Out."

"Can I come back later?" Chad asked.

"We'll see." There was no promise in Jones's words.

Chad left the room reluctantly. He had everything to be grateful for. Nella was recovering. His face fell as he saw Nix sitting in the outer office.

"Still sore?" Nix asked.

Chad's face was unhappy. "You dig too hard, Evett."

"Maybe," Nix said noncommitally. "But this is damned important to me. If you knew how much time and effort I've spent in running Doolin to ground . . ." He sighed and didn't finish. He eyed Chad speculatively. "Nella come to?"

"What makes you ask that?" Chad asked evasively.

"The way you looked when you came out of that room. And Jones didn't look worried."

"She came to."

Nix waited a long moment. "Did she have anything to say?"

"Some," Chad admitted.

"Tell me."

Chad shook his head. "This job is mine. I swore I was going to get that bastard. I'm going to do it."

"Chad, listen to me. Washington has been on my tail for so long that I don't know what it's like to wake up in the morning and not have them there. I lost some good men because of Doolin. Can't you see —"

He stopped as Chad continued to shake his head in that slow, decisive manner.

"God damn it, Chad," Nix exploded. "This is not a one-man job. What if I refuse to let you go?"

Chad unpinned the badge on his shirt. "You can't stop me," he said flatly.

Nix handed back the badge. "Put it back on," he said wearily. He tried a new tack. "I don't think Nella even saw him."

Chad grinned tantalizingly. "She saw him all right."

"And she told you where to find him?"

"I know where to look," Chad replied.

Nix shook his head. "I never knew you to hog all the glory before."

Chad's face turned savage. "You think that's why I'm doing this?"

"No, I don't," Nix admitted. "But this is as important to me as it is to you. Maybe even more. I'm thinking of protecting a state. You're only thinking of getting revenge."

Chad turned those words over in his mind. Nix might have something there.

Nix thought he saw a weakening in Chad's face and pressed harder. "The more men I can throw after him, the greater chance of success I'll have."

That obstinate look was on Chad's face as he shook his head. "Like you did in Ingalls?"

Nix winced. "You still believe a lone man will have a greater chance?"

"At least Doolin won't see a mob coming after him and make a run before they even get close."

Nix's face was red, and they were on the verge of a serious quarrel. He breathed hard. "Don't you realize Doolin will cut you down before you can draw your next breath?"

"Is your being along going to stop that?" Chad asked heatedly.

"It might, Chad. Do you know where he is?"

Chad gave that some more thought. Nix wasn't his enemy. Both of them were on the same side. "Not exactly," he confessed. "Nella mentioned a farm I never heard of."

"I could be of some help," Nix said softly. "I know all the country around Ingalls pretty well. I've got the same reason as you have, Chad. I only want to see Doolin dead."

Chad turned that over in his mind, then gave in. "Nella told me she saw him at the Ellsworth farm, northwest of Ingalls. That mean anything to you?"

Nix bobbed his head. "It certainly does. I've been out to the Ellsworth place a couple of times looking for Doolin. He wasn't there. I felt like those old folks out there would do anything to protect him. How did Nella pick out that farm?"

"She was raised there. She's a stepsister to Edith, Doolin's wife. She figured there was a good possibility that they'd get together. She used her head, and she was right. She talked about a small hill east of the farmhouse. She lay out there three days watching the place through field glasses."

Nix slapped his knee, his eyes shining with admiration. "That proves Doolin followed her back to Guthrie with the sole purpose of getting rid of her."

"I don't see how you figure that," Chad objected.

"I'll bet she used those glasses in the late afternoon. The sun reflected off them. Somebody in that farmhouse caught the flashes of light. I'm guessing Doolin investigated and found Nella was gone. He's as wary as a wild animal. He had to stop her before she could tell anybody where he was. What a gal. She almost made it back here."

Chad thought of the agonized hours waiting for Nella to regain consciousness. "She almost didn't too," he muttered.

"Agreed," Nix said soberly. "But I think now he can go back to that farm and feel secure that nobody knows where he is. Do we go and get him, Chad?"

Chad grinned savagely. "You're reading my mind. But I've got to talk to Nella again."

"Sure. I didn't plan on leaving in the middle of the night."

Doolin wanted to put Lady into the barn before Edith saw her. The mare was literally weaving on her hooves. Edith would raise pure hell when she saw the mare.

"So you finally got back," said a voice from behind him.

Doolin whirled, and his expression was guilty. "Hello, Edith," he drawled. "I was putting Lady away."

Edith came around him, her eyes suspicious. "You were going to put her away without telling me you were back?"

"Aw, Edith. You know better than that," Doolin said.

Edith took the reins from Doolin's hand and

271

led Lady to a patch of sunlight coming in through the sorry roof. "Oh my God," she wailed. "She looks terrible." She turned, accusation written all over her face. "You rode her off her hooves. And you were going to put her away without doing anything for her?"

Doolin had never seen Edith so angry. "Aw, Edith, I had to, to catch up with that bitch. At that, I almost missed her."

The angry glint faded a little in Edith's eyes. "Did you get her?"

Doolin nodded. "At almost the moment she stepped off her horse. I got her while her young man had his arms about her."

"You're sure?" Edith insisted.

Doolin impatiently shook his head. "Did you ever know me to miss? I didn't hang around to check. The smartest thing I could do was to get out of Guthrie as quick as possible."

"Then you don't know for sure whether or not she's dead?"

There was that questioning of his marksmanship again. "I know," he said positively. "I saw the way she fell. Don't you see, Edith? I can come back here and rest in peace. Nobody knows where I am. Can't you see how much that means to me?"

That appeal got through her anger, and she melted against him. "It means a lot to me too," she murmured before she lifted her face to his. She had her man back with her for a good, long time.

She broke away from his embrace. "Now, you do something for Lady," she ordered.

"What can I do?" he complained. "She needs rest most of all."

"You can rub her down," Edith said crisply, "before the stiffness sets in. I'm going into the house and mix some bran in her oats and warm it up."

"All this bother," Doolin complained. "She's just a horse."

"She's Lady," Edith said furiously.

Doolin gave in. "If she doesn't recover, I'll buy you another horse."

"It won't be Lady," Edith said stiffly.

Doolin sighed and set to work scrubbing down Lady's weary muscles. If he wanted to get back in Edith's good graces, he'd better do everything he could for this animal.

CHAPTER 22

Jones and Mrs. Moore came out of the rear room just as Nix and Chad finished talking. Chad jumped to his feet. "Can I talk to her now?" he asked eagerly.

"Always the same damned question," Jones said sourly. "You cannot. She fell asleep before she finished the bowl of soup." He relented a little as Chad's face fell. "Try again in the morning. Nella's recovered so well, I don't think her sleeping periods will be as long. For God's sake, go on back to Mrs. Tucker's and sleep in a decent bed."

Chad glanced at Nix. Nix nodded and said, "He's making good sense, Chad."

"All right," Chad said reluctantly. "I'll be back in the morning."

"Not at daybreak," Jones shouted after him as he went out the door.

Nix walked down street with Chad. "Go on and get some sleep. I can still make arrangements for a good horse for you tonight." He paused, frowning. "I probably won't be able to buy any supplies until morning. It doesn't matter. We're not in any race. I'll be by for you at eight in the morning."

Chad nodded. He watched until the night swallowed up Nix's figure. Originally, he had been determined that he would go after Doolin alone. Perhaps it was just as well that he would have an older, experienced head with him.

Mrs. Tucker had to shake him awake in the morning. Chad frowned at her. "It can't be eight already," he said pitifully.

"It is," she said firmly. "I'm doing just what you asked. Marshal Nix is downstairs waiting for you."

"Tell him to give me a few minutes," Chad said. On second thought, he decided on a shave. He hoped to see Nella this morning.

He walked downstairs, and Nix looked at his shining face. "Good lord. You took time to shave! Did you think you were going courting?"

Chad grinned. "Hardly. But I did plan on seeing Nella before we go."

Nella was still asleep when Nix and Chad walked into Jones's office. Chad knew how hopeless it was trying to see her before she woke. "Do we have time for breakfast?" he asked.

"I imagine you can squeeze it in," Jones said sardonically. He shook his head as Chad walked out with Nix. Damnedest pest he'd had on his hands for a long time.

They went back to the restaurant Nix had recommended. "Better get something solid," Nix suggested. "It could be your last good meal for a long time."

Chad ordered steak, fried potatoes, and a slab of apple pie. It might be odd fare for breakfast, but he was hungry.

"I see you brought your Winchester and pistol with you," Nix commented halfway through the meal. "I brought plenty of ammunition for both guns. Now, all we'll need is stuff we can cram into our saddlebags."

Chad chewed a moment in reflection before he asked, "Evett, how do you figure this?"

"I honestly don't know," Nix said solemnly. "I've been up against him so many times. He's as slippery as an eel. He's always found a way to slip out of my hands."

"He won't this time," Chad asserted.

"I wish I was as positive as you are," Nix said gravely.

They finished the meal, and Chad paid the

woman a dollar. Outside, he patted his belly. "As good a meal as I ever ate."

"Something good to remember for quite a while," Nix said. "You think Nella is awake now?"

"We can go see, Evett."

They walked into the doctor's office. Jones looked up from his desk and shook his head. "I knew I wouldn't be able to go very far without seeing you."

"Doc, is she awake?"

"She woke just a few minutes ago. Mrs. Moore is in with her right now. Do you suppose you could give her a few moments to get Nella ready for the day?"

Chad ignored the sarcasm. "Then I can see her?" he insisted.

"I wouldn't get rid of you any other way, would I?"

Chad grinned. "You wouldn't."

The waiting was like all the other times: long and tedious. "Doc, I think I'll have to be away. Something that has to be done. Would that hurt Nella?"

Jones was in a sour mood this morning, and he showed it. "Do you think you can claim any credit for her recovery?" he asked in a biting tone.

Chad didn't flinch. "I think I can.

277

Seeing me meant something to her."

Jones threw up his hands in complete surrender. "You may be right," he conceded. "You go ahead with your trip. Just be sure she knows about it. I don't want her being disappointed when you don't show up."

"She'll know," Chad promised.

Mrs. Moore came out and smiled at Chad. "I just finished combing her hair. She looks brighter than I've ever seen her."

"Can I go in?"

Mrs. Moore glanced at the doctor, and Jones said, "Let him go in. He won't stop pestering us until his wishes are granted."

Chad grinned mockingly at him. "You're all heart, Doc."

"Oh, get out of here," Jones said explosively.

Chad walked into the room, and Nella smiled at him. Mrs. Moore was right. She had never looked better. He crossed to her and took her hands. "How are you feeling this morning?" he asked gruffly.

"I hope you haven't come to ask me to a dance," she said, her eyes dancing. "If you haven't, then I feel pretty good."

He bent and kissed her forehead. "You're a wonder."

"Is that the best you can do?" she reproved.

He kissed her lips, still gentle. "Is this better?"

"Some," she admitted. "But I'm hoping one of these days you'll do better."

"You can count on it," he said gravely. "And that's a promise."

Some inner emotion made her eyes shine like stars. "I won't be here forever," she whispered.

"And I won't be gone forever," he said in the same serious tone.

Her eyes widened, and she gasped. "You're going after Doolin," she exclaimed.

"Don't argue against it, Nella," he said evenly. "It's something I have to do."

She bobbed her head. "I know, Chad. But be so careful. He's deadly."

He gave her a twisted grin. "Don't you think I've learned that? Nix is going with me. He thinks that doubles our chances."

"I'm so glad," she said, her voice shaky.

He bent and kissed her again. "Look for me when you see me coming."

She clasped him hard, despite the wince it put on her face. "I'll be praying for you every minute."

Chad walked into the outer office. "I'm leaving now," he announced.

"Nobody's crying," Jones said. He changed that. "Unless it's Nella. You didn't upset her, did you?"

Chad shook his head. "She knows what I'm doing. Ready, Evett?"

"As ready as I'll ever be," Nix grunted.

They walked outside, and Chad looked at the horse Nix had picked out for him. It was a big rangy roan, and he had fire in his eyes.

"Has he got bottom?" Chad asked.

"More than you'll ever need," Nix assured him.

Chad mounted and put a long look on the doctor's office.

"We'll be back before you know it," Nix said gruffly.

"I'll kick your butt all over town if we aren't," Chad said.

Nix grinned. "Then I'd better see that we make it safe."

Chad nodded gravely, his thoughts on the girl in that rear room. "Yep."

CHAPTER 23

This was a hell of a lot better trip than the first one Chad had made to Ingalls. In a wagon, it had been much slower and more uncomfortable. They were making good time. Darkness was beginning to creep up from the earth, and Chad guessed they were fifteen miles from Ingalls. He had speculated curiously about what Nix would do about the town, but he supposed in due time Nix would tell him. It hadn't been a talkative trip, for each man was busy with his thoughts. Most of Chad's thoughts were centered on Nella. Right now, he didn't think he was the luckiest man in the world because he was occupied with this trip. But all this stress would pass, and he and Nella would pick up where they had left off before she was wounded.

Nix held up a hand, and Chad reined his

horse over to him. "Think we've made enough distance for the day." He looked questioningly at Chad, and Chad nodded. "Suits me." He wasn't exactly hurting, but a stiffness was creeping into his legs. It would increase with a few more miles until he was virtually crippled.

Chad dismounted, stripped off saddle and bridle, then hobbled the horse. This was flat country and he didn't see trees of any kind. He wondered why Nix had picked such desolate country.

Nix hobbled his horse. He bent over the saddlebags and pulled out two cans. He grinned at Chad. "Won't be the most comfortable camp in the world."

Chad took that as a challenge. "I can stand it," He didn't say what he had in his mind. He could stand anything Nix could.

Nix opened the two cans and handed one to Chad. "We don't want to light a fire," he said. "A fire could be seen for a long way. Somebody might get curious enough to investigate."

Chad shrugged. He would have liked to have a cup of coffee, but he could do without it. It was a good thing the weather was mild. A man couldn't take an Oklahoma winter without warmth.

He sat beside Nix, but there wasn't a real sense of companionship between the men.

That damned Doolin had caused the necessity of all this change in routine, he thought in quick irritation. He finished his can of peaches, drained the juice from the can, then flung it from him.

"I'll get you another can if you want it," Nix offered.

Chad considered the offer, then shook his head. "No, that'll do. Are we going straight into Ingalls, Evett?"

"We'll make a wide swing of it," Nix replied. "This has been Doolin's country for a long time. A lot of the people around here knew and supported him. I doubt if that feeling has had enough time to die."

Chad nodded. He felt a little better. Nix had a good head, filled with the hard lessons of experience, and that gave Chad a feeling of security.

"How far is the Ellsworth farm?"

"We should reach it by dark tomorrow," Nix replied. "We'll look the farm over the following morning and see if Doolin's there."

"And if he is we go in after him?"

It was too dark for Chad to see the gesture, but he had the feeling Nix shook his head.

"We do not," Nix said sharply, confirming Chad's impression. "I know that hill that Nella used. All we do is confirm Doolin's presence, then get the hell out of there."

"Why, damn it?" Chad started to protest.

"There's at least four people in that farm-house," Nix said. "All of them willing to do everything they can to protect Doolin. Do you want to go up against that many guns?"

Chad thought about it, then said slowly, "No, I guess that wouldn't be wise."

Nix grunted his agreement. "We didn't come up here to get involved in a gun fight." There was something about the tone of his voice that told Chad he was thinking of the Ingalls raid.

"You didn't come all this way to just *look* at Doolin," he challenged.

"We came up here to see Doolin. Remember that hill Nella talked about?" He paused, then said reflectively, "I know that hill. We'll use the back side of it to get to the top. After I'm positive Doolin is there, we'll slip away."

He chuckled at the strangled sound Chad made. "There's a hamlet about five miles out of town. It's too small to even be named. But it has a grocery store and blacksmith shop. Doolin has to buy some supplies. That hamlet has to be his choice. When he rides to it, we'll take him there."

Chad let out an explosive sound of relief. Nix was an old dog, but he knew all the tricks. "Did you bring glasses?"

Nix snorted at the uselessness of the question. "We'll be on that hill at dawn. The sun will be at our backs. There'll be no flashes of light to give us away. As soon as we know for sure he's there, we'll take up a new position outside that little hamlet."

"How much waiting is that going to take?"

"Who knows?" Nix answered. "Regardless of how much time it takes, it'll be worth it if we can take Doolin without a shootout. You better get some sleep now."

Chad stretched out, then said, "I can't tell you how grateful I am. If I came up here alone I could have run into one hell of a mess."

"I've had a lot more experience, Chad," Nix said gently. "It takes a lot of years for a man to learn." He must have fallen asleep almost immediately, for his soft snoring came on the heels of his words.

Chad lay awake a while longer, his mind picking through a lot of thoughts. He thought of Nella, Bill Doolin, and of himself. He guessed he was one lucky man to have Nix picking a way for him. He fell asleep on the last thought.

Nix shook him awake. "You planning to sleep your whole life away?"

Chad yawned and stretched. "Not too much

of it," he grumbled. The sun wasn't fully up yet.

Nix handed him another can, already opened.

Chad looked at it with distaste. "A man could get enough of this in a hurry," he growled.

"Ain't it the truth?" Nix agreed. "But it fills you up. After it's down, you don't have to eat anymore."

"I could take this cold canned food," Chad remarked, "if I could only have a cup of coffee to go with it." He hadn't really looked at the can Nix handed him, and when he did he yelped in disgust. "Cold beans for breakfast! That's really eating on the lowest level."

Nix grinned his amusement. "It slips down without much effort."

Chad flung his can away before it was finished.

"You ain't suffering yet," Nix said unfeelingly, "to throw away good food like that."

They gathered up the hobbled horses, and Chad was swearing before they found them. Even a hobbled animal could cover a remarkable distance during a night if it kept up those mincing, persistent steps.

Chad caught his horse first. "You damned hammerhead," he said in rancor. He walked the roan over to where Nix stood.

Nix was still amused at the disgust in Chad's face. "One bad thing about horse riding," he said. As Chad's eyebrows went up, he finished, "Makes him complain about the slightest amount of walking."

Chad thought about that, then laughed. "How right you are."

About noon, Nix pointed to his left and said, "Ingalls lies in that direction about five miles."

Chad looked, but he couldn't see any sign of a town.

Nix guessed at what was in his mind. "It's not a very big town."

"I guess not," Chad said shortly.

"Just pray that nobody sees us out here," Nix said seriously. "If any word got to Doolin, everything we've done so far would be washed out."

"Do we look like lawmen?" Chad asked.

"We don't have to look like lawmen. Just the news of a couple of strangers in the country could send Doolin scooting."

Chad shook his head. He hadn't thought of that.

The country grew more sparsely settled. After passing the vicinity of Ingalls, they saw only a few farmhouses. Chad noticed that Nix gave every one of them a wide berth.

They didn't stop for lunch, and Chad didn't

care. Just the memory of that breakfast would last him for a long time.

Toward evening, Nix said, "We're getting close."

"Close to what?" Chad asked crossly. As far as he could see, this was empty country.

"The Ellsworth farm," Nix replied. "Our timing couldn't be better. We'll tie our horses pretty far away from that hill, then climb it after dark. Maybe by morning we'll know whether or not Doolin is still around."

"I've waited a long time for that," Chad said grimly.

CHAPTER 24

Chad thought dawn would never come. They had crawled up the hill during the night and flattened out against the ground. If there was a farmhouse around he couldn't see it.

As the light strengthened, Nix had a pair of field glasses in his hands, studying a shabby house that slowly materialized out of the night mist.

"He won't be up now," Chad remarked.

"You're probably right," Nix replied. "But I want to catch a look at the first one who steps out of that house."

Chad studied the distance between the house and the hilltop. "Maybe we could get a shot at him from here."

"Too far," Nix grunted. "If we miss he's gone, then there's all this to do over again."

"I wouldn't want that," Chad said moodily.

289

Ever since he had heard the name Bill Doolin, he had known nothing but trouble. The sooner that first night was removed from his thoughts, the better off he would be. Gradually, Chad could feel the warmth of the sun on his back. Waiting was always acute; this waiting time seemed more so.

"Ah," Nix said softly.

The single syllable alerted all of Chad's senses. He could see that a figure had stepped out of the house, but at this distance he couldn't pick out any details. "Can you see who it is?" he asked in a guarded voice.

"He's got a beard," Nix said softly. "That's new. See what you think." He handed the glasses over to Chad.

Chad studied the man in the glasses. He had never seen any more of Doolin than just a picture. The beard changed his appearance. "I don't know," he said miserably. He drew in a sharp breath. "Wait a minute," he said softly. Edith had just stepped out of the house. Chad knew her well. Edith walked over to the bearded man and briefly hugged him.

"It's him," he exclaimed. His voice vibrated with satisfaction. He handed the glasses back to Nix.

"That Edith?" Nix queried.

"No mistake," Chad grunted.

"Then it's got to be him," Nix said positively. "By God, Chad, he's here."

Chad could appreciate how Nix felt. He knew that the same quiver of excitement ran through him. "What's our next move, Evett?"

"We wait until they go back into the house, then snake off this hill. I don't want to risk the slightest movement up here being seen. We can scurry down the rest of this hill when it's between us and the house. Then we get our horses and ride to that little hamlet and wait."

Chad groaned at the prospect of another wait. "How long do you figure that'll be?"

Nix shrugged. "It could be a considerable time. I never knew of a farmhouse that wasn't well stocked. But no farm can stock staples such as sugar, coffee, and salt. Sooner or later, they have to purchase those things."

"Do you figure Doolin will go out for them?" At Nix's nod, Chad said, "There's something wrong with that figuring. He could send somebody else."

"Yes," Nix agreed with a mirthless flash of his teeth. "It's a risk we'll have to take. But I've got a strong hunch it'll be Doolin." He was looking through the glasses again. "They've just gone back into the house. We can start backing off this hill."

They stayed close against the ground as they

moved off the skyline. Chad felt sure that nobody could have seen them.

They were halfway down the hill before Nix said, "We can straighten up now."

Chad stood and brushed the dust off his clothes. "I wouldn't recommend this to anybody as a way of traveling," he said sourly.

Nix grinned. "I wouldn't recommend quite a few things about our way of life."

They walked a good mile before they reached the tethered horses. "Hungry?" Nix asked.

"Some," Chad admitted.

"Can you hold it back until we get safely out of here?"

"I won't die," Chad grunted.

Nix chuckled. "I hope you're a good prophet."

They mounted, and Nix led the way. He knew where that small hamlet was. This was all alien country to Chad; he didn't have the slightest idea where they were, or where they were going.

He judged they had ridden a good five miles when Nix's upraised hand stopped him.

"The hamlet is just ahead," Nix said. "We sure don't want anybody there seeing any strangers around. I've got a suspicion that all the people there have a strong sympathy for Doolin."

Nix selected a small wooded knoll. "This may be your new home for quite a time," he warned.

"It can't be ended too soon for me," Chad said unhappily.

Nix laughed. "You know, I feel the same way."

They tied the horses on the far side of the knoll. "I don't think anybody passing by will see them," Nix commented. He took four cans out of the saddlebags. He opened them and handed two to Chad. "A real banquet today," he said and grinned.

Chad looked at his two cans with open dislike. One was beef, the other tomatoes. "Damned if this wouldn't break a man of the habit of eating."

"You thinking of that, Chad?" Nix laughed.

"Maybe," Chad said. He got most of the food down; it seemed to sit on his stomach like a lump.

"You'll forget all about it in an hour or two," Nix said. He gathered up the four cans and, using a hunting knife, dug a small hole and buried the cans. At Chad's look of surprise, he said, "Tin cans don't belong here. If somebody did catch a glimmer of light from them they might look closer."

"You talk like these people have special

293

senses," Chad said sourly.

"Maybe they do," Nix answered seriously. "They're simple people living the same way. Maybe that puts them closer to the wild. Don't underestimate them," he cautioned. He uncased the glasses and put them to his eyes. "Good view," he said and handed the glasses to Chad.

At first, Chad didn't see much. The knoll put them above a dirt road, and it seemed to go no place. Then he saw where it apparently ended at a ramshackle store, next to another building that looked on the verge of tumbling down. "Not very prosperous." He gave the glasses back to Nix.

"The people living around here are dirt-poor," Nix said. "I don't know how either store stays in business. The little time I spent around here, I didn't see a dollar's worth of business being done in both places."

"And you think Doolin will come here?"

"I said he might," Nix corrected. "I don't know of anyplace where he can buy supplies for miles around."

They lay and watched the hamlet the remainder of the day. Chad counted four people going into the grocery store. A horseman rode up to the blacksmith shop, and a wagon lumbered up just before darkness.

"How do they make a living?" he asked incredulously.

"I told you these were poor people. They don't require much." He sighed as he recased the glasses. "Another day gone, and we're no closer to what we came for. You hungry?"

Chad's stomach rebelled at the prospect of having to face another can. "I guess I'd better eat," he said slowly. It wouldn't make any difference what Nix handed him. It was just something to fill up his belly.

They could watch the road without glasses, and Nix said, "He's got to come this way. This is the only road in here."

"If he comes at all," Chad said unhappily.

Nix nodded. "There's always that possibility. I told you that before we left the farm."

Chad's unhappiness grew. "I know." Maybe Doolin was one of the lucky men; maybe they would never run him down. He thought of the vow he had made to himself and Nella. He wasn't going to weaken because one day hadn't been fruitful.

A few lights came on in the hamlet after darkness. Somehow those lights made Chad even lonelier.

"Let's move closer to the road," Nix said. "I've got a hunch if Doolin ever comes it'll be about this time."

They lay just off the road where their ears could help their eyes. Any traffic passing this way would certainly be seen as well as heard.

They waited until well past midnight before Nix said, "We'd better move back up." Chad's silence spoke eloquently of his disgruntlement. "I told you quite a while back that it takes a lot of patience to make a lawman."

"You did. And I'm still here," Chad said in surly voice.

Nix didn't speak again until he said, "Better get to sleep while you can. It's going to be a short night."

"I wish I thought the same about the days," Chad replied. He lay there, thinking of the few lights he had seen come on in the hamlet. Lights would be on in Guthrie. He wondered how Nella was and if she was thinking of him. "Not at this hour," he admonished himself, and closed his eyes.

Nix woke first in the morning, and he shook Chad. "Maybe it'll happen today," he tried to say brightly.

Chad's nerves were scraped raw, and he snapped at Nix. "You don't believe that any more than I do," he snarled. "Forget that, Evett," he apologized. "But damn it, don't you ever sleep?"

"I slept," Nix replied calmly. "What I miss

on this job I'll make up later."

Three fruitless days passed in a row, and their food was running low.

"Maybe I could go into that grocery store and buy a few supplies," Chad suggested.

Nix considered that, then shook his head. "Even if they didn't know you you're still a stranger and suspicious because of that. No, we'll drag it out until all our food is gone."

Chad's eyes glazed. "You mean just give up and leave?"

"You got a better idea?" Nix asked coldly. "I'm still not partial to starving, and we can't live off this country."

Not a dozen words passed between them the entire day. At dusk, Nix handed Chad an open can and said, "That's it."

Chad remembered how he had cursed these cans of cold food. He wished he had all of them back. He'd have more respect for them.

They moved down to the road, and Nix said, "Let's work our way closer to the grocery store. I've got a feeling this is going to be the night."

At Chad's jeering, he said stubbornly. "After you've been in this business as long as I have, you get a feeling how things are going to turn out. I've got that feeling tonight."

There was a thick clump of sumac not fifty yards from the store. "Can we work our way to

297

that sumac?" Nix asked. "If he does come tonight it'll cut the range down."

"I don't see anybody around," Chad answered. "Want me to go first?"

"Take it easy," Nix cautioned. He waited until Chad had wriggled into the clump of brush, then joined him. He was breathing hard, and he whispered, "Not old age. Just excitement."

Chad nodded. He could believe that. Both of them had their Winchesters and, at this distance, their fire should be deadly.

Looking through the stalks of the foliage, they had an excellent view of the grocery's front door. Chad lay there, and the thought in his mind became a constant refrain. "Let it be tonight," he prayed over and over.

Not a half hour had passed before Nix gripped his arm, and his fingers had a bite. "Hear that?" he whispered.

Chad started to shake his head, then caught the sound of an ancient vehicle, for it creaked and groaned. One wheel was in bad need of axle grease, and its squeaking set Chad's nerves on edge.

The wagon passed them, and only a driver sat on the seat.

"What do you think?" Nix whispered.

Chad shook his head. He didn't know. The

light was too poor to make a positive identification. They watched a man clamber down from the seat. He carried a rifle in one hand.

"Whoever it is, he's ready for trouble," Nix said softly.

Chad's excitement was mounting. "I think it's him. I know a way to find out."

He crawled out of the sumac, and Nix's grabbing hand missed him.

The figure was moving up the few steps to the store's entrance, and Chad cut the distance to less than forty yards before the man entered the store.

He stood and called, "Bill. Wait up." Doolin wouldn't know his voice, but the hail should have results.

The man whirled, and his natural wariness took over. He peered uncertainly at the figure at the edge of the road, and his rifle came up in his hands.

Chad didn't wait any longer. The man had reacted instinctively to his name. It wasn't the most solid identification in the world, but it had to do.

Chad pulled the trigger of the rifle. He heard a harsh, sobbing grunt, and knew the bullet had hit its target. Doolin had tremendous vitality for the bullet didn't knock him down. He got the rifle butt against his shoulder, and

Chad fired again. He pumped in bullet after bullet, and behind him he heard Nix firing rapidly too. That weak identification must have satisfied Nix.

That terrible rain of bullets knocked Doolin back several steps. Even then, he struggled to fight back. At that, he got off a bullet that whistled sharply over Chad's head. Then he began to fall, slowly. He fell like a great tree that had been deeply undercut and, for an instant, Chad thought he might make it. He kept firing until his magazine was empty. Nix was still firing.

Doolin finally fell, tried to crawl, then flattened out, his hand still reaching out for something he could grab hold of.

Nix joined Chad, and he was breathing hard. "He was tough," he said soberly. "Until the last, I thought he might claw his way out of the fight."

After the crashing reports of the rifles, the stillness was unearthly. Chad commented on the stillness. "I thought everybody within earshot would be rushing out."

Nix shook his head. "You don't know much about human nature. These people have been through gunfire before. They'll just try to burrow a little deeper and wait until they're sure it's all over. Let's go see what we've got." At

Chad's questioning look, he said harshly, "Nobody will contest our approach."

They walked up to the still figure. Doolin lay on his back. Even without moonlight, Chad could see the moist, dark patches on his clothes. Doolin had been riddled like a sieve. He had lost his hat, and his rifle lay a good yard from him.

Nix squatted for a closer inspection of that distorted face. "Even with that beard, it's Doolin. Help me put him into the wagon."

Doolin was a heavy man, and death made his weight hard to handle. His body was so loose, so inert. Chad took hold of his legs, and even there he felt something moist and sticky on his hands.

Nix took the shoulders, and was audibly panting by the time they had deposited the body in the bed of the wagon.

He glanced at the store, and still nobody had appeared. "Fear's still holding them. Let's get out of here. You drive. I'll jump off when we come to that knoll and go up and get our horses. I won't quit sweating until we put a good piece of distance between us and here."

"That makes two of us," Chad said dryly.

He made a wide swing in turning the wagon, and his body was rigid in anticipation of a fusillade of bullets aimed at them. But the little hamlet remained quiet. The last thing Chad saw of it was lights burning in that godforsaken place.

He drove down the road, only slowing down enough so that Nix could safely make his jump. He whipped up a weary team into great speed. At any instant, he fully expected to hear outraged cries coming from behind him and the sound of angry people in pursuit. He didn't slow down until he was around a bend. He stopped the team and waited until Nix appeared, riding his horse and leading Chad's.

The raw smell of fresh blood must be strong coming from the wagon for Nix had to fight the horses to get them close to it. He was cursing fluently by the time he got the reins firmly tied to the wagon's tailgate.

He climbed up beside Chad and said, "We can get out of here now. Maybe a faster speed will knock some of the nonsense out of those fool horses' heads."

Chad slapped the reins on the rumps of the horses and got them into a lumbering run. The motion of the wagon sent the body rolling from one side to the other.

"Slow it down some," Nix advised. "We don't want to throw him out."

"You still think it's Doolin?"

"I'd bet my reputation on it," Nix answered.

"Why did you want to bring him along?"

"There's some reward money out for him," Nix replied. "I figure we might as well collect it."

It wasn't a pleasant thought, collecting money for a body, but that was the way life was. Chad didn't object. "You figure this smashes the Wild Bunch."

Nix shook his head in denial. "It might scatter them when this news gets out, but that's about all. They've lived too long outside the law to change. Only two things will change those kind of people: what happened to Doolin, or a long jail sentence. Doolin was the brains of that bunch, and they'll be lost for awhile. One of these days, you'll see their heads pop up. You still want to be a lawman?"

Chad thought about that for a long moment. "Yes," he answered slowly. "Somebody has to get rid of that kind of people." He was silent again. There would be tears shed over Doolin's death. Edith would cry her broken heart out over the loss of her man. Nella might shed tears of relief over the disappearance of her threatener; those were the right kind of tears.

"The reward money the only reason you're bringing him in?"

"No," Nix answered slowly. "I want his body put on display for the public to see. It may cause some wild kid to stop and think before he starts on the same road. I'm glad you decided to stay with me, Chad. You proved a lot to me in this."

Chad grinned. "I'm thinking of getting married. A married man has to have an income, doesn't he?"

"I'm glad you've got enough sense not to let that gal get away," Nix said. "You'll never do better."

"Don't you think I know that? Where are we heading?"

"To Stillwater. We can leave Doolin there. As riddled as he is, he'll draw a lot of public attention."

"You don't regret the way it was done?"

"Why should I?" Nix asked in mild astonishment. "You set out to kill a rattlesnake, and you don't quibble over the way it's done, do you?"

"I guess not," Chad replied slowly. His voice strengthened. "Hell, no. You do it any way you can before it can strike you."

He sank back into his thoughts. It would take some time to reach Guthrie, but it wouldn't be long before he saw Nella again. He was unaware that he was humming a little tune.